THE POWER

"Give me the bag Maria."

She looked shocked. "No! Don't you understand? This is power! You see? *I can control you!*"

It was weird. Suddenly I found myself at her side, the knife was no longer in my hand. Then she pulled the mask out of the bag. The gold and silver on it sparkled in the sunlight and the ringing in my ears grew louder. She was bringing the mask up to her face and something in me shouted that that was terribly wrong. She shouldn't do it.

"Maria, don't! For God's sake, don't!"

The Okora Mask

By

Rex Wiseman

LEISURE BOOKS **NEW YORK CITY**

A LEISURE BOOK

Published by

Dorchester Publishing Co., Inc.
6 E. 39th Street
New York City

Copyright © MCMLXXIX by Tower Publications, Inc.
1984 by Dorchester Publishing Co., Inc.

All rights reserved. No part of this book may be reproduced or transmitted in any form or by an electronic or mechanical means, including photocopying, recording or by any information storage and retrieval system, without the written permission of the Publisher, except where permitted by law.

Printed in the United States of America

The
Okora Mask

1/Africa

"It's an interesting piece, Excellence." I set the heavy bronze figure down on the table between us. "It represents a Dahomeen chieftain or king bringing home a captive, probably another chief. Notice the big difference in the size of the figures. That's to emphasize the power of the winner."

The Spanish ambassador shifted in his chair and impatiently tapped the ash from his Havana cigar. "The history doesn't interest me, *M'sieu* Loring." His French rolled out like marbles in a dishpan. "Is it authentic? Is it old? Is it valuable?"

I picked up the roughly cast hunk of metal again, turned it over thoughtfully, eyed the green and brown corrosion that covered it. "Well, it's authentic, all right. I mean it certainly comes from

Dahomey and no doubt it was made by a Dahomeen. As for its age... that could be anywhere from five years to six months. The normal way to age a piece like this is to douse it in battery acid and bury it for a few months." I put it back on the table and leaned back in my chair. "I'd say it's worth about six dollars on the open market."

"Ah, the pig!" The rest of the Havana was ground to shreds in the ashtray as the diplomat stood up. "Three hundred dollars he asked, that flea on the ass of a donkey. He should go to prison for that!"

The flower of Spanish culture was already at the door, so I got up to open it for him. I felt sorry for the poor Hausa trader who was only doing what any used car salesman back in the States might do. "Tell you what, Excellence. When you've finished with the trader, send him over to me. The piece isn't worth anything, but it does have a certain style about it that I like; from an artistic point of view, that is."

He hesitated, looked straight at me. I let my eyes shift for a brief second and smiled innocently. His face became a sunbeam. "Of course, *M'sieu* Loring. Just as soon as I've finished with him. *Au revoir*."

"*Au revoir*." Sucker. With hard bargaining he might get it now for a hundred. Pleased with myself, I did a little dance out to the terrace that overlooks my city. The buildings sparkled in the smog-free air. The sky was as blue as Swedish eyes and the sea was a brilliant turquoise. Clouds from a Chinese painting drifted over a deep green landscape. Yup, Dakar is really a sexy city. Just a peninsula sticking into the Atlantic from the west coast of Africa; capital of Senegal, but not really part of it; it's pure sex.

And I, my friends, am impure sex. I call myself, as the French so aptly say, Leland Loring. It doesn't ring true, you say? Since this is my story we'll play it my way or I'll take my typewriter and go home.

I've been living in Dakar for about five years and I love it. As cities go it isn't very big, but it has a healthy share of beauty, mystery, intrigue, ugliness, wealth, misery, corruption, kindness, excitement, murder, treachery, folly, and fun. In other words, it's filled with human beings. When some people hear it called the "Paris of Africa" they laugh because of its small size, few restaurants, fewer hotels, and lack of entertainment. But the amenities are not what it has in common with Paris. The French have imbued it with a charm that has captured the imagination of all of Black Africa. It's the center of culture, everyone gets a lifetime job in the government, and every day is a holiday. The reality, of course, ranges from shocking to beyond all expectations.

What captured my imagination five years ago were the women: Nubile Lebanese lassies, wise and witty French *demoiselles,* proud and fashion-conscious Senegalese, and even an occasional wide-eyed British or American tourist. Beautiful women, cute women, lovely women, pretty women, amorous women. I'm actually rather fond of women. They're so female.

On this particular joyous day that I am writing about, my thoughts were once again (or still?) running in this philosophical vein as I leaned against the railing, gazing dreamily at the city and idly rubbing my thumb over the polished wood of a *minsereh* figure from Sierra Leone. I realized gradually what I was doing and turned to appraise the rest of the collection displayed on the terrace. Pieces that ranked me as an expert in African art by friends, clients, and several museums.

On my left was a huge moorish chest decorated in brass, silver, copper and gold. On a shelf attached to the wall behind it stood several pairs of exquisite *ibeji* dolls (if I don't tell you they were exquisite who will?), and further on was a finely carved *chiwara* antelope ready to leap into space. Over by the door was a tall *Senufo* statue of a fertility goddess... strange how certain objects will bend your thoughts onto a totally unrelated path. For some odd reason I began thinking of my very private Lebanese secretary, Aletha. Strange also, how some thoughts can be so intense they attract the subject, because through the same door undulated my mental vision. Brown-haired, brown-eyed, brown-bodied Aletha. I felt a quick pity for all the girls in the world who had only learned to walk. When Aletha undulated beside another girl who merely walked, the latter invariably looked clumsy. Aletha flowed like lava, she was liquid and warm as mulled St. Emilion (1950). An uncontrolled glance from her could burn out a man's brain, and her voice, a whisper of distant thunder, made one's spine tremble.

The afternoon was hot and Aletha had on a flimsy yellow mini-dress that would have given her life imprisonment in Madagascar, where the police run around measuring the distance from hem to knee. She purposely stood between me and the descending sun and a shiver rose up the back of my neck. She moved toward me. I put a hand on the railing to steady myself as she spoke.

"There are no more appointments today, Monsieur Loring."

Although I can be debonair and casual with any other woman, Aletha always makes me feel like I'm standing naked on a stage. The problem is that, in matters sexual, my iron-clad will power fades into ocean spray when Aletha is on the make. That she was on the make now was indisputable. She kept coming toward me until her chest touched mine. She was a threat to the undergarment industry. In the States she would be picketed by the unions. With a devastating pout she unbuttoned my shirt, slipped her brown arms inside and around, and flowed against me, filling every crack and crevice. Like capillary action, I thought. My hands eased down her back and attached themselves indissolubly to her delightful derriere. I have a theory about derrieres. I call it the Loring Bottom Proposition. You see, every girl at birth is allotted a certain amount of a mysterious force which I call Driving Power. Its visible manifestation usually appears from about age sixteen, but its duration follows no pattern which I have been able to discern as yet. An expert (I am one of the privileged few) can tell by the size and shape of the girl's posterior appendage just how much of the magical quality she has. This, of course, has nothing to do with her ability to use it. In most cases the Power is only potential until proper training and grooming have brought it to full bloom. A rare few seem to have an innate knowledge of its employment, which brings into doubt the theories of the environmentalists, but in any case, a proper application of the theory will avoid many wasted hours for the true researcher. The power cannot be taken for granted, however. In other words, it is not a constant. A few centimeters either way can destroy the delicate balance necessary for the ideal Drive. Readers who are interested in further study may refer to my upcoming fourteen volume work on the subject, with case studies.

Where was I? Oh, yes. Soldered to Aletha. Well, we were just getting primed for intensive action when a cool, mocking voice came from the open terrace door.

"Am I intruding?"

My basic Puritan ethic made me attempt disengagement procedures, but Aletha's arms held me like a vise. She turned to the intruder and hissed steamily.

"The office is closed for the day."

Aletha's glare would have turned an ordinary mortal to stone. Obviously the creature who had spoken was not an ordinary mortal, since she didn't oblige. Tall, with jet-black hair and dignified beauty, she was Artemis the Huntress watching the carryings on of the plebians with amused tolerance. Aletha felt the condescension and the prick of her fingernails in my back presaged an Olympian battle between Artemis and Aphrodite that would rock the peninsula. With a casualness that brought a flicker of admiration to the lovely visitor's eyes I recommenced my intimate caresses and spoke with the tone I use at my desk.

"I'm afraid I'll be in conference for the rest of the day. I should be back in the office by ten tomorrow or, if it's urgent, perhaps I could get in touch with you this evening."

She grinned wryly. "It's very important, but not urgent enough to interfere with your conference. I'll be at the Snack Bar of the N'Gor Hotel at eight tonight." She turned to go, then paused to look back as Aletha's dress floated gently to the floor. "I do admire a man who lets nothing interfere with business," she ended softly.

Dakar by night. The heavens were salted with scintillating stars and the growling Atlantic surf beat steadily on the tropic shore (please save your applause for the end of the book). I sat at the bar of the exotic spot known as *"Le Snack Bar"* of the N'Gor Hotel, on the edge of N'Gor Bay, across from N'Gor Island and next to the village of N'Gor, and sipped my drink. I'm sorry it wasn't a very special drink whose detailed concoction I had carefully described to the bartender, expecting to berate him for adding three slivers too much of ginger or something. That might have made interesting reading for all you trendseekers, but the bartender serving me knew only two drinks: Gin and tonic and whiskey and soda. If you think it would help, I could tell you that the whiskey was scotch (don't ask me what brand) and the soda was Perrier, which is good for the kidneys. You can't say I don't try to please. Now, the snack bar was fairly empty, it being a Monday night. An old, white-haired European was sitting some distance away and directly in front of me was a table of sweet swingers with short skirts. I was resting my weary eyes among their knees and thighs and feeling very wise when what to my surprise... Okay! If you wanted to read poetry you'd have bought a book of poems, right? Right!... a damp hand took me by the chin and turned my head around. Artemis. Or a sea nymph. Remembering my mythology I rather hoped it was a sea nymph. Two black bits of nothing kept her from being technically nude. Her black hair hung in curls and made fascinating patterns on her shoulders. Her eyes sparkled from the soft bar lights and her luscious lips were moving back and forth, up and down. How long had she been talking to me?

"...and to introduce my colleague, Dr. Carlos Aliberti. Dr. Aliberti is a specialist in Saharan archeology from the University of Milan." Her colleague turned out to be the old geezer I had noticed before. He was almost a caricature of a professor, with a white, droopy moustache, faded blue eyes, and clothes that might have been handed down from his grandfather, who was taller than he. I shook his leaf-like hand briefly and turned back to the nymph. "My name is Maria Benedetti. I'm also an archeologist, a student really, a pupil of Dr. Aliberti. Let's sit down and we'll tell you why we came to you."

We trooped over to the nearest vacant table and I held Signorina Benedetti's chair while she gracefully sat down. It gave me a chance to get a good look at her boobs. Oh, man! I dig beautiful young Eyetalians. I sat between them, Maria and the doctor, I mean, signaled the waiter and ordered a round of Cinzano and soda. After three false starts we finally got them. "So you are both archeologists.

What do you archeologue?"

Maria looked at me unbelievingly for half a second, mentally labeled me a true, blue dunce, and explained. "An Archeologist, Mr. Loring, studies the past by means of the cultural remains of ancient civilizations. At one time the Sahara was green, with many animals and people who in several ways had a very advanced culture. The sites of several important cities have been found, but so far hardly any organized excavation has been done. There is one site in central Mauritania called Aoudaghost which was the subject of an intensive study by Dr. Aliberti. Until recently his findings were accepted as correct. About five months ago, however, a team of Americans went in and now they are claiming that every one of Dr. Aliberti's conclusions was wrong!"

At this point the professor burst out of his cocoon. "They are fools! Liars! Just because they have fancy equipment; just because they are *Americans* they think they can destroy my proofs, destroy my whole reputation!" The old boy was frothing at the mouth. The girl spoke a few words in Italian which calmed him down somewhat. He huffed, puffed, and fell silent, with the outraged look still on his face.

"Dr. Alberti can get so very emotional," she apologized.

"Don't you ever get emotional?" I asked. Her eyes widened slightly and I thought I could see hints of hot sparks flashing. Or maybe it was just a reflection from the lamps.

"I try never to get emotional about my work, Mr. Loring."

"What do you get emotional about?" I'm a persistent bastard.

"We are here to talk business, are we not?" A mocking smile softened the words.

I leaned back and swirled the ice in my drink. "That's what you say. But what do you need from me? I'm just a dealer in African art."

Maria put a cool hand on mine and looked at me pleadingly. "Mr. Loring, we've come to you because we know you have influence with certain Mauritanian officials. If time were of no importance we could just go through normal channels and wait for permission, but the next international conference on archeology is only three weeks away and we need time to gather our data and prepare it for presentation. Your name was given to us by Romano Fiore in Rome. He said you were the only person who might be able to get us in and out in time." I did a mental double-take at the mention of Romano's name. Last I heard he was serving time for murder in Naples. She went on. "Perhaps you aren't aware of what can happen when serious doubt is cast on a scientist's major work. His whole career is put in doubt. His enemies attack all his other theories and pick them apart like gleeful vultures! If Dr. Aliberti can only refute the Americans' claim by pointing to his findings of ten years ago, he'll be laughed out of the conference." Her eyes had begun to blaze a little and I found the effect very stimulating. Both her eyes and her voice softened as she continued. "However, if he can furnish data and samples even more recent than the Americans', the psychological effect alone will be tremendous!" I was still trying to decide whether I preferred her eyes blazing or soft when I realized they were waiting for me to comment.

"Um, yes, well." I wildly tried to recall what she had been saying. "You, uh, said that Romano put you onto me, huh?"

"Romano Fiore, that's right. I met him in Rome only a few days ago. We had been in touch with the Mauritanian embassy in Paris, but it was obvious our request would go nowhere. I was complaining to a friend at a party when Mr. Fiore joined our conversation. When he heard our problem he suggested we get in touch with you."

"So you flew right down here for a chat."

Dr. Aliberti boiled over again. "I do not like the tone of your voice, Signore. We were in desperate straits. There was nothing we could do in Rome or Paris. Our own Embassy could do nothing to help us because the Mauritanians are angry about my country's attitude toward Yemen. Did you know that our consulate in Nouakchott was almost stoned?"

"Oh, yes. I heard about that. The police wouldn't let the mob stone yours, so they went and stoned the Germans. That must have been a surprise. All right, so you're desperate. You'd have to be to come to me. Now, you'd like me to use my famous influence to get you to Aoudaghost. Let's say for the sake of argument that I could do it. That would mean I'd have to take personal responsibility for you and wipe your noses all the way there and back. That's worse than a bad trip on mescaline. At this time of year it would be pure misery for you and anyone else you drag along. I have a lot more interesting things to do right here in Dakar."

The professor stood up trembling. "We are not asking to 'drag you along'!" I could almost see the static electricity shooting out from his whiskers. "You were the one who imposed that condition. All we need is permission to get in and a guide to lead us to the site and back. We are used to uncomfortable situations. I myself have spent months in the desert under the most extreme conditions. If you refuse to help us that is your affair. Your name was given to us in good faith, but if you are afraid or unwilling for whatever reason, then we can only try our best to work through the Italian embassy. I am an old man and I am tired of all this talk that seems to get us nowhere, so I am going to bed. If anything at all is ever decided you can tell me about it in the morning. Goodnight!" With a final grunt he stalked away toward the long stairway leading into the hotel.

We stared after him for a few seconds. Then Maria smiled at me. "I apologize for Dr. Aliberti's rudeness."

"No reason," I said pleasantly. "Are you staying here?"

"Yes, it's comfortable and convenient." She paused. "Is there no way to change your mind? We are willing to pay quite well."

"Change my mind? I never said I wouldn't do it. I just said it wouldn't be any fun."

"Then you will do it?" Her hand was on mine again.

"Not for free, sweetheart. What are you willing to pay?"

"Name your price." Her voice was firm.

"Five hundred thousand dollars."

She choked on her Cinzano. "I thought you were going to be serious!"

"I am. This is Africa, don't forget. We bargain for everything. Since I'm selling, it's my duty to inflate the price. Your job is to beat me down to a price that makes us both unhappy on the outside and wildly elated on the inside. Now, what's your counteroffer?"

She was silent a moment. Then she chuckled and said, "Ten dollars."

I laughed so hard I almost fell off my chair. An hour and several drinks later she had driven me down much further than I had driven her up. I always was lousy at bargaining with beautiful women. For ten thousand dollars I would take them to Aoudaghost and back. Actually, the price both elated me and worried me sick. For two weeks of pulling strings and babysitting it was a lot of bread. That was great. But it was too much bread for an archeologist to be tossing around. Even for the sake of a career. Furthermore, no self-respecting archeologist would be caught dead—no, that's not the right word to use—would want to be seen in the company of Romano Fiore. Trouble was in the offing and I tingled with anticipation.

I started to order a drink to celebrate our agreement, but Maria begged off and rose from the table. "I've already had more than I'm used to and I must get some sleep. How long will it take for you to arrange our entry?"

"Oh, about two days. And I'll need your

passports. I suppose you'd like me to arrange transportation? Okay, I'll hire a plane and inform the authorities of our arrival. We'll need a Land Rover to get us to the site. I'll send one off tomorrow morning. It should be at Tamchakett in about three days. That's where we'll land the plane. Barring complication, we can leave three days from now and be at the site the day after. I assume you have all your own equipment?"

"Yes, we do. When do you want the passports?"

"I'll send someone by tomorrow morning at eight. By the way, I'll want half my fee before we leave. And all expenses are extra."

"That will be fine. I'll give you a check tomorrow."

I took her arm and we walked into the hotel and up to her room. Like the worldly gallant I am, I bent to kiss her goodnight. "Save that for your secretary," she smiled as she ducked away and out of sight. I suppose I could have knocked down the door, but what the hell. She couldn't run away from me in the desert.

2/Dakar

The night was still in its youth, so first I stopped in the lobby of the hotel and called my Lebanese associate, Sami, a man with more contacts than a prescription lens manufacturer. "Sami, old friend, old buddy, old pal, paisano, amigo, ami..."

"You want something big?"

"How did you ever guess? We are off on a new adventure!"

"I already have a date."

"*Tres, tres drole.* There are other things in life besides women. Not many of them as interesting, I admit, but this one has possibilities. I have just been hired by two Italian archeologists. By coincidence, one of them happens to be a beautiful young woman..."

"I already have a date."

"Stop interrupting. Besides, she's mine. I got first dibs. Anyway, they want to go to Aoudaghost for a few days and are paying super-high wages to get there. I want you to send Souleymane to the N'Gor tomorrow morning at eight to pick up their passports; load Salif into the big Land Rover with a week's provisions and ship him off to Tamchakett to arrive in three days; hire a plane to carry six passengers for Friday; get entry permits for two weeks on the passports; and inform the Prefect at Tamchakett of our arrival."

"How do you get involved in these things so fast?"

"That's what yoga training does for you. The names are Carlo Aliberti, supposedly a prof from the University of Milan, and Maria Beneditti, who looks too pretty to dig around ruins. Call Rome and check them out. Also, they said Romano Fiore gave them my name."

"I thought he was doing time."

"So did I. They said they met him at a party. If Romano was there it must have been a wild one. They're paying me ten thousand U.S and that's way too much. Not for my talents, for the service. The deal smells like the sewer at Soumbedioune. Methinks there is more than dirty old potsherds drawing them on."

"I'll check it out and let you know tomorrow. *Ciao.*"

"*Ciao.*" Well, now what? It was still early. Should I call Dominique and go dancing? Take Caroline out for some late drinking? See if Suzanne wants to smooch? I decided to try something new and different. I went to bed alone."

Next morning I popped in at the office to take care of some correspondence and pinch Aletha on the behind. Business wasn't quite booming. There was an order from California for several gross of leather belts, necklaces and fake talismans; a couple of museum orders for various rare masks which I would have carved and prepared immediately; and other odds and ends. Needless to say, the income from art exports wasn't sufficient to pay for my particular life-style. The real money came from my services as a professional adventurer, called a soldier of fortune in the old days. In a continent as politically mixed up and economically unstable as Africa I had no trouble in finding work. Usually there was more than I could handle at one time. Being an art dealer was a convenient cover-up since it gave me a good excuse to travel. Of course, I was known by the secret police everywhere, but for the most part the jobs I took were on the side of one government or another, and borders are not too terribly difficult to cross with a little care. My free-lance situation made me available for a wide variety of work and I made it a cardinal principle to guard a fierce loyalty to whomever I was working for until the job was done. After that, naturally, I was up for grabs. The work was often dirty and dangerous, but lots of fun in a way. For me, it was a game of skill. So far I had more or less won, but I knew the day might come when the odds against me would be too high. It didn't worry me. I look upon death as a new adventure. When it comes I'll play the game, but until then I'll play the game of life. I was allowed to use Dakar as my headquarters only because I had promised never to take a job against the government of Senegal.

At the moment, however, the only thing I had going was the guided tour to Aoudaghost. There being nothing in particular to do until Sami called, I kissed Aletha goodbye and went sailing.

Three hours later I was mooring my *Requin* when the boat-boy called out from the dock. "Monsieur Loring! You have a telephone message."

I waved my thanks and took my dinghy in. I went to the club lounge and the bartender told me that Sami had called, and wanted me to come to his office.

Sami's office, or rather group of offices, was (were? Damn grammar anyway!) in an ugly yellow building on Gambetta Avenue. Fat market women wearing incongruously beautiful robes squatted on the sidewalk to sell hot peppers and kola nuts, while their bare-bottomed children rolled in the dust. I turned into a dark stairway and climbed two flights between and around kids and dogs and dirt. I knocked at a nondescript door which opened and let me in to a stark white hallway. Sami's third son greeted me in Arabic and showed me to the door at the far end of the hall. I opened it and stepped into an airconditioned dream.

A thick green carpet covered the length and breadth of the rectangular room. The wall behind me and those on my right and left were panelled in knotty pine. The ceiling was criss-crossed with rafters and the far wall was entirely given over to a filmed scene of a brook slithering through a clearing in a forest of lofty pines. From time to time a bird would flit across the scene, an early morning sun catching the color of its feathers. A few feet in front of the scene was an immense desk covered from one end to the other with papers. Around a stone fireplace on the right-hand wall were some easy chairs and in one of these sat Sami, waiting for my reaction.

"Now this one I really like. Much better than the monastery you had last week." I walked over and sat beside him.

Sami grinned his pleasure. "Yeah, that monastery got to be too much of a drag. All those monks walking back and forth. I even got so I was singing aloud with the choir." He offered me a cigarette, but I declined and pulled out my corncob.

"So what's the news from Rome?"

"According to DiAngelo, Aliberti is a well-known archeologist at the University of Milan, and he did publish some work on Aoudaghost. Maria Benedetti comes from a wealthy family and is a student at the University studying under the professor."

"Well, I guess that takes care of my suspicions."

"Not quite. You said they got your name from Romano. Romano is dead."

"Somebody get him in prison?"

"No, he was paroled a week ago. Two days later he was killed by a hit and run driver on the Piazza Esedra in Rome. The police found a one-way ticket to Dakar in his pocket."

"The plot thickens. Any reason to suspect more than an accident?"

"Nothing really tangible. Romano's mother said he went to the Piazza to meet someone. She didn't know anything about the trip to Dakar."

I leaned back and puffed. Why would Romano come to Dakar? And so soon after parole? To see me? I have a magnetic personality, true, but I was partly responsible for sending him to prison. For revenge? Equally unlikely. Romano knew the risks of the trade. On a job? Very, very probable.

"Try to find out who Romano was hanging around with and what he was doing just before he got out. Also, what he did the day after he got out."

"I already checked that."

"You're so efficient it's sickening. Well?"

"He wasn't hanging around with anyone in particular, but about two weeks before his parole he received a visitor. A pretty young woman who gave her name as Evangelina Moretti. She brought him a book." He paused for dramatic effect. "The title was, 'The Destruction of Aoudaghost,' by Carlo Aliberti."

I bit through my bit. Romano could barely read. Why should he suddenly take up archeology? "What else did you find out?"

"The day after Romano was released he went to a party in a posh section of Rome. Definitely out of his class. That's all we know about him. As for the story the scientists gave you, it seems to check out as far as it goes. There was a group of Americans digging at Aoudaghost recently and there is an international conference of archeologists due to take place in a few weeks. The passports appear to be authentic, but we need more information from Milan to make sure, and that will take time."

"Try to get it just the same. Is everything set for the trip?"

"All set. Salif left this morning and the passports will be ready to pick up tomorrow. Who's going to fly the plane? You?"

"Don't make it sound like such a dangerous idea. I might. No, on second thought I'd rather have my hands free just in case. See if Rene or Philippe are available. Have you put a tail on the diggers?"

"No, but I will if you say so."

"Probably be a good idea. Get Demba to use one of his men. Tell him I'll stop over his place tonight around midnight."

"Who are you seducing this evening?"

"Please! Don't be so crude. I am escorting a young lady of good standing to dinner at the Brazilian Embassy."

I picked up Dominique at eight that night. She was the daughter of the first secretary of the French Embassy and a ravishingly pretty girl.

Let me enter a note of explanation at this point. You may be saying to yourself "Oh, brother, another beauty. Doesn't this guy ever meet any dogs? It just isn't plausible for a guy to always be meeting and going out with beautiful women. Let's have a little more reality."

To put the record straight, I do meet women who are unattractive. In fact, most of the women I meet are unattractive, or at least not what you would consider beautiful (though there's no telling what your taste might be). The salesgirl I bought a shirt from the other day had a nose that was too big. The woman who runs the flower shop has squinty eyes. The daughter of the American ambassador leaves me cold and I wouldn't date any of Sami's nieces on a dare. So why would I write about them? I date beautiful women by choice, and I meet beautiful women by chance. I promise you, though, the first fascinating ugly woman I meet, I'll write about.

As I was saying, Dominique was ravishing. She was about twenty, with long black hair, and long tan legs. Tonight she wore a swirly, black silk affair that ended at mid-thigh and put a lump in my throat. *"Fantastique,"* I murmured in her ear as I led her to my car. *"Tu es le soleil de mon coeur, la reve de mes nuits... viens vivre avec moi sur une ile tropicale..."*

"Oh, Leland," she laughed, "you are so funny!"

I suppressed an urge to punch her in the nose, and tried to close the door on her foot, but she was too quick for me. Nothing deflates a man like a woman who laughs at his words of love.

As we drove along the Corniche I guarded a huffy silence until she leaned over and blew in my ear. "Leland, cheri, what would you do if I said, 'Yes, my darling, take me to your island now and let us love a thousand times ere rises the morning star'?"

Very seriously, I answered, "I would definitely laugh." We were still giggling as we walked into the embassy grounds.

The new Brazilian Embassy was built only

recently. It faces the sea, but like most private residences in Dakar it is completely walled in and the only view is from the upstairs bedrooms and terrace. We greeted the ambassador and his wife at the entry. I had sold them some good pieces and paid a courtesy call on some of their relatives once in Rio, so we were slightly more than just acquaintances. Dominique, of course, knew them quite well.

We passed on across the lower terrace and into the garden where drinks were being served. Three other couples were already there—the American deputy chief of mission and his wife, the Moroccan charge d'affaires and Madame, and the Turkish ambassador and ambassadress. I ordered drinks from a white-clad Guinean servant (the choice at diplomatic affairs is nearly always limited to scotch and soda or gin and tonic, unless the occasion also calls for champagne. The Americans will usually add bourbon and the more imaginative hosts will include vodka. Just thought you'd like to know.) We all conversed in French for convenience and were discussing the latest African adaptation of Hamlet when our hosts joined us with the last two guests. I admit I was surprised to see Maria and the old prof.

After an hour or so of conversational gambits we went inside for dinner. Couples are invariably split up, so I found myself sitting between the hostess and Maria.

"I would have expected to see you with the charming girl I saw you with in your office."

I raised my eyes from her low-cut decolletage to see her smiling. "With my secretary? It isn't done. I only play with Aletha during working hours."

"Oh, was that play? I thought it was more serious."

"Well, work hard, play hard, you know. What have you been doing for amusement?"

"The professor and I have no time for play." My eyebrows went up and she blushed a tiny bit. "I mean we have work to do. We spend most of our time at the museum checking the archeological studies of the French."

At that, Madame Brazil broke in and the conversation turned to archeology in general and remained there for the rest of the evening. My art business requires a fairly detailed knowledge of the subject and I listened closely for the answers the prof and Maria gave to various questions. I even threw in a few of my own, but not too many, since I felt it better for the moment not to let on how much I knew. There were no earthshaking revelations. As far as I could tell the professor really knew his business. Maria, on the other hand, was obviously what she said she was—a student. Her knowledge could have been picked up in a week of good reading.

After dinner, we took our cognac (for digestive purposes only, insist the French) and split up into small groups. I corraled Maria at one end of the terrace to tell her the passports were ready and would be sent to the hotel in the morning. And to tell her that the plane was arranged. And to tell her that her dress was stunning and her eyes were bewitching. I was just getting around to dinner the next night at my place when somebody stepped on my instep.

"OWOWOW!" I hopped to the railing and leaned against it, one foot held not too gracefully in both hands.

Dominique was at my side, cooing in French. "Oh, *cheri,* I am so sorry! I also must have been bewitched by her eyes and so could not see where I was walking."

I laughed and cried at the same time. It was my fault. I disobeyed one of my own rules: Never make a date with a woman when you are still with another. But she almost broke my foot with her spiked heel. "I forgive you, darling," I lied. "Let's get out of here and make up."

By this time everyone was staring in our direction and the hostess had run up to us. "Are you all right, Monsieur Loring? What happened?"

"Nothing, nothing serious. I'm all right. An old soccer injury. It'll be all right, but I think we should go. Thank you very much." Brushing aside polite protests, Dominique and I said our goodbyes and she helped me limp to the car. Fortunately, I could still stand the pressure of the clutch. We drove in silence along the Corniche until we neared the turnoff for her place.

"Why are you slowing down, cheri? Are you still angry? Did I hurt you that much?" She leaned over to kiss my cheek.

"It is just possible that I may live, my love, but I am definitely not in the mood for fun and games. I have to see a friend about some business. I'll call you in about two weeks."

"Two weeks? You think to punish me. Are you going back to see that Italian?"

"Not tonight. I'm going home to soak my foot. Day after tomorrow I'm off to Mauritania. I'll call as soon as I get back. Honest."

"You think I will be waiting? You think I have nothing to do but wait until you call? I shall go dancing every night. I shall sleep with a dozen different men!"

We were in her driveway. I reached across and opened the door. "Don't catch anything, sweetheart. *Au revoir.*"

"*Merde!*" I watched her until she reached the door. I loved the way she swung her bottom when she was mad.

A few minutes later I was knocking on the door of Demba's pad in the Sorano Building, a combination state theatre and apartment house that was built for the African Arts Festival that Duke Ellington starred in. The door opened and I spoke first. "N'diaye, *Ngadeff*!"

"Loringa, *diamareck*!" We clasped each other's right thumb and exchanged the ritual pleasantries in Wolof, his native language. Demba N'diaye was a model Senegalese. Big, handsome, pitch black, all French on the outside and pure African within. He used to work for the Security Police, but now ran his own private practice. We had been partners on many an escapade and had stopped counting the number of times we had saved each other's lives. We were friends and equals. In all but one respect, which I never allowed myself to forget. He had royal blood.

"Let's sit down and I'll tell you about my latest adventure."

"Start talking. I'll get something to limber up your throat. Cognac?"

"Fine, but I'd like it with coffee." I settled comfortably in an armchair. "Let's see, it all started with a beautiful woman."

"I would have been surprised if it hadn't."

"Don't interrupt. Once upon a time there was a lovely princess who was also an archeologist." I told him the whole story, including the part about Dominique's heel on my foot.

"What do you intend to do?"

"About the trip to Aoudaghost?"

"No, about your foot."

"I shall probably soak it in champagne. That wasn't the point of my story, however. The two tomb-robbers seem clean, but I don't like the connection with Romano. I have managed to stay alive thus far mainly by not believing in coincidences. I'm sure this trip to Mauritania has an ulterior motive. As a novice in illegal doings, I have come to seek the advice of an expert in things criminal. What say you, Sherlock? Any exciting happenings in the African underworld?"

"If you are a novice, my friend, Al Capone was a seminarian." Demba took a sip of cognac and looked throughtful. "There is the usual stuff going on. Diamonds coming through here from Sierra Leones and Ghana. White slave rings are still in full operation." He chuckled. "Isn't it amusing that forcing black girls into prostitution is still called white slavery? Counterfeiting, drugs. Everything is happening. Nothing spectacular enough for your tastes, as far as I know. Still, if I hear of something that might have to do with your trip, I'll let you know."

"By carrier pigeon? I'll be in the desert day after

tomorrow. Oh well, maybe something will happen between now and then. I hate to think of spending two whole weeks in Aoudaghost with nothing to do but trying to seduce Maria."

"Don't ask me to feel sorry for you," he laughed.

We continued talking until nearly one in the morning. Demba invited me to spend the night and I was tired enough to accept. I took the spare bedroom and left the door open to catch what little breeze might accidentally lose its way during Dakar's muggy June nights.

Someone was in the room. No sound occured to let me know it, but I was quickly drawn out of the depths of sleep to an awareness that someone was there. As was my habit, I lay naked on top of a single sheet in the middle of the bed. Without opening my eyes, I knew that the 'someone' was standing by the right hand edge of the mattress. Raising my eyelids by the barest fraction, I could make out a black belly button staring out of a muscular black belly. With a feeling of relief I thought it must be Demba and was about to sit up and ask him what was wrong when my subconscious cried out, "No! It's A Stranger!" In the next instant three sounds broke the quiet of the night: "Ssssst!" "HAAAH!" "Oulk!"

The first was the sharp intake of the intruder's breath, which came at the same time I saw his belly muscles contracting. The second sound was a scream tearing out of my lips as my left hand flew over my body to bury its stiff fingers into his solar plexus toward his spine. The third was the surprised death gurgle of a man wondering what had gone wrong.

By the time I was on my feet Demba was in the

room. He flicked on the light. The attacker lay on his back with his arms still clutched around his middle. He was big, impressive even in death. Thick leather bands hung with small leather squares encircled his biceps. Around his waist a tight leather cord decorated with strips of red cloth bit into the dark flesh. Demba knelt down and looked closely at the man's face. Sighing, he leaned back and said softly, "Poor Papa Seck. I wonder how much you paid the marabout for those amulets? And I wonder how much you were paid for this? You should have stuck to your wrestling." He glanced at the finely honed machete which had fallen on the bed. "Lee, he could have sliced your head clean off with that thing."

I slipped into my clothes with trembling hands. I can kill when I have to, but I don't like it. I also don't like to be that close to death. "For a second I thought it was you. It must have been that amulet around his waist that warned me. It must have been designed to protect him only against steel."

Demba picked up the machete and walked back to the door. "Let's find out how he got in. There may be somebody waiting for him." He turned off the light and we moved into the living room.

There was no need to look very far. The French doors were standing wide open and a slight breeze shifted the curtains in graceful patterns. Even from inside we could see the cord hanging from the balcony above Demba's terrace. Demba gestured for me to cover the door to the upstairs apartment while he climbed the rope. The rope was of nylon, knotted at regular intervals. Demba tugged to make sure it was still secure, and began pulling himself up hand over hand. Seven stories below a worn-out car coughed along the otherwise lonely street. If Demba had twisted himself around he could have admired the blazing lights of Boulevard Charles de Gaulle pointing like arrows toward the Independence Obelisk in the distance. He didn't do that, of course. He just kept climbing steadily until a hand touched him on the shoulder. From his shoulder it went under his arm and helped him to a position where he had one leg swung over the cement railing. Then the owner of the hand suddenly changed his mind and tried to use the same hand to persuade Demba to descend all the way to the street without an elevator. For his efforts he received a heavy fist in the mouth that sent him reeling back to the floor. Demba scrambled the rest of the way over and leaped on the man before he could recover. He tried to struggle, but Demba's ebony fingers closed around the man's neck and his mouth opened and shut like that of a fish out of water. By the faint moonlight Demba could see he was a *metis* and about his own age. Easing his grip the slightest bit, Demba asked in a whisper if anyone else were in the apartment. The man shook his head feebly. The detective listened very carefully without being able to detect the least sound from inside, and eased up a little more.

"What's your name, little boy?"

"Gomez. Please don't kill me!"

"Who are you working for, Gomez?"

"I can't breathe. Let me breathe. I can't talk."

"I don't like to repeat my questions, Gomez. Say hello to your ancestors for me."

"No, no! I'll tell. A *toubab* hired us. An American.

He said he'd pay us well if we'd get rid of Loring."

"What was his name?"

"I don't know." Squeeze. "I really don't, I don't!"

"Then you're not much use to me, are you, Gomez?"

"Please! I know more! He had yellow hair. With a moustache. He said he was a sailor. We didn't ask any questions. It was a lot of money."

"Where did this little meeting take place?"

"At the *Taverne due Port,* two days ago."

"*Two* days ago? Are you sure of that?"

"Two days, that's right. I swear it!"

"Why did you wait till this particular night?"

"The toubab told us to wait till he gave the word. Last night he said it would have to be this morning early. He gave us the key to this apartment."

"Hmmm. I have a lot more to ask, Gomez, but this isn't the place. You're coming with me. If you make any noise or try to get away I'll kill you on the spot, understand? All right, let's go to the door." Together they went through the apartment to the front door where I was waiting.

Now is the time for the more observant among you readers to ask how I can describe what happened above when I was standing in the hall. This is called literary license. Also, I might have ESP, for all you know. Don't forget who's writing this story. Bear along and don't be so picky.

To continue at the point where you so rudely interrupted me. The three of us went back down to Demba's apartment and dragged Seck's body out of it and into the service elevator. Demba turned to me. "I'll get rid of the body and then go wake up my staff to see if we can get any more information out of this goat's tit here. You try and get some sleep."

"Sleep? How am I supposed to sleep? I'd kind of like to know why someone wants me killed, too, you know."

"Look, Lee, you are an expert in some things and I am an expert in some things. I don't hang over your shoulder while you work, so grant me the same favor. I'll meet you on Goree Island at the Espandon tomorrow—no, today—at one o'clock and tell you all about it. 'Night."

I protested. "But-but-but!" Too late. I was in the hall and the elevator door was closing. I went back into the apartment, carefully checked all the doors and windows, and tumbled into bed for a brave attempt at slumber. To my surprise, I did sleep for about ten minutes. But in that time I dreamed that I was being sliced into tiny bits by a giant buzz saw and being fed to a monster whose face was hidden behind a curtain. I suppose you can call that sleep if you want to.

3/Goree

Eight-fifteen the next morning. The typewriter is clacking away busily. The outer door opens and in walks... "death warmed over, Monsieur Loring!"

"Yes, Aletha, thank you very much, that's just what I need. Now cook up a pot of coffee, get me Sami on the phone, and cut out the cliches until after lunch." Stomp, stomp, stomp. The inner door opens and Leland Loring gropes his way to his cool, leather couch where he flops with a groan. What a HELL of a night!

"Sami is on the phone, Monsieur." Aletha was peeking through the door. "You'd better..."

"Yes, I know. Close my eyes before I bleed to death. Thank you, Aletha. Goodbye."

"Was she..."

"Shut up, *cherie,* and get out of here, will you?" The door closed. I gathered up my various limbs and crawled to the desk. Using my tremendous power of mind over matter, I succeeded in picking up the receiver. "Hello, Sami? I want you to give me a rundown on... No, I am not talking with my mouth full of rocks! Just be nice and tell me what my clients have been doing. Italy, huh? New York? Interesting. Who did they talk to? Oh, that's too bad. You think they might have used code? Well, why would they call New York to talk about pottery? Could be. Who did the calling? She would. Have they spent any time at the museum? Hmmm. What was she doing? Which beach? Did she meet anyone? Ha! I guess I'd have tried to pick her up, too. Still, one of them might have been a contact. I know, Sami, I know, but I stay alive by being suspicious. I've got a story to tell you later on about that. Who's going to pilot the plane? Good, I trust Jean-Pierre. Does the Prefect know we're coming? Well, keep trying. I'll be in touch this evening. Ciao."

That chore out of the way, I hung up, stripped, and headed for a hot shower. In case you are wondering, my office not only has a bathroom, but a bedroom attached. You never know when one or the other will come in handy. I abandoned myself to the sensual pleasure of soap and water, tempered with thoughts about Signorina Maria Benedetti. It was hard to imagine her as an archeologist. I'm not saying that beautiful women can't be scientists, but isn't it unusual for them to go around looking like a model for a fashion magazine? My thoughts skipped. Who wanted me dead and why? I couldn't think of any great secrets I had that anyone would have to kill me to get. I'm a reasonable man as long as I'm not on a payroll. I mused in this way until a voice behind me raised goosebumps on my neck and turned my gut to stone.

"Hi, Tarzan!"

Without turning around I began to pray aloud. "Please, dear God, don't let it be true. Please, Heavenly Father, let it be a nightmare. If you do that for me, I promise I'll go to church every Sunday for the rest of my life!" Tinkling laughter destroyed the possibility, so with ice in my heart I turned to face the menace that had just thrown back the shower curtain. An objective observer, besides finding it hard to be objective, would have had a difficult time understanding the dread I felt on seeing the marvelous creature now gazing on my naked wetness. An abundance of copper-colored hair surrounding her pixie face gave an impression of adolescence that contrasted sharply with a hedonist's bod. The above-mentioned objective observer would have taken in her boots and her half a dress and would likely have felt that here was a sweet bit of fruit ripe for the plucking. He would have been dead wrong. In fact, if he made the wrong move he would be just plain dead.

"You don't seem happy to see me, Lee," she pouted.

"About as happy as I'd be to find a snake in my sandwich, Darla." I shut off the shower and reached for a towel. "So what are Satan's sisters up to now? Who's side are you on today? Rubbing myself dry, I paid no attention to her bold appraisal of my nudity.

Why should I withhold that little pleasure, after all?

"You're still in pretty good shape, except for those bruises you've got here and there in unmentionable places. How did that happen?"

"Answer my question first, viper. What are you doing here and for whom?"

"Oh, I'm just sort of on vacation. You know how it is, sometimes. You have to get away from it all, get a breath of fresh air and all that. So I figured I'd look you up and we'd have a ball together. Fly off somewhere, just the two of us, and sock it to each other for old time's sake." She picked up a green bottle from the shelf above the sink, unscrewed the cap, and sniffed. "Karate? My, you are a brave man." Putting the bottle down, she gave me a prurient little smile and wandered into the bedroom.

I swore by some Norse gods I know and wrapped the towel around my hips. What was up? That bitch never stirred a muscle without a damn good reason. The last time she played up to me I ended up in a hospital with four broken ribs and a dislocated shoulder. She'd been on my side, apparently, until she unexpectedly threw me off a bridge in northern Ghana. Then she'd had the gall to send flowers and apologies from London, two weeks later. She could at least have paid the hospital bill. What fiendish trick was on her mind now? For the time being I didn't want any part of her schemes. I had enough to do with the diggers. Darla was no doubt waiting for me to go into the bedroom where she could charm me into making love. Let her go to hell. I'd get dressed, show her out, and forget her. It would be a lot easier if she were eighty years old, but I could do it and I would!

I stepped back into the office where a pot of hot coffee was waiting. I poured a cup of the thick, bitter stuff (a French specialty) and forced it down while reminding myself to have a talk to Aletha about letting in stray animals. Nonchalantly I drifted into the bedroom. I had to get dressed, didn't I? Darla had laid out my things. A tan bush suit. Socks and sandals. And a pair of leopard patterned briefs.

"I found them at the bottom of your drawer. I think they're adorable."

I sat down on a chair. "Look, Darla," I began.

Darla came up behind me and gently rubbed my shoulders. "What took you so long?"

"Your mother called. She said you forgot your broomstick."

"Good ol' Mom," she chuckled, coming around to the front of the chair. "Always looking out for her little baby." She stopped directly in front of me with her legs slightly spread and her hands on her hips. "You know, you look delicious, sitting there like that."

"Go away, ugly, or I'll brain you. I don't have time to play games. Besides, I'm all worn out. I couldn't play if I wanted to." I started to get up, but Darla leaned over and put her hands on my shoulders. I closed my eyes and gritted my teeth. Here was one of the sexiest women I had ever met practically begging me to make love, and here was I, the great lover, doing my best to avoid it. You may be asking yourself, What kind of stoop is this guy, anyway? Friend (I'm assuming the best), Darla is also the most dangerous woman I have ever met. Next to her, Lilith was a Sunday school teacher, Jezebel a P.T.A. vice-president, Salome a girl scout, and Mata Hari a den mother. Getting into Darla's loins is the ultimate in pleasure, but the results are always disastrous. So that's why I said, "I'm serious, get the hell away from me."

She leaned over farther, resting her forearms on my shoulders and locking her hands behind my neck. Then she spread her legs wider and straddled my lap. I didn't dare push her off, because I didn't dare touch her. But I was determined not to let myself give in. I was damned if I'd play stud just to please her. I smiled inwardly at the thought of her disappointment when she realized just how strong my will could be. She began to cover my face with kisses and my will grew stronger than ever. I had just about reached the point where I was ready to pick her up, toss her on the bed and laugh at her frustration when she whispered in my ear. "Hey, Lee, babe, you know what? I forgot to put on my underwear this morning."

"You what?" It came out as a gurgle.

"Yeah, isn't that funny? Just forgot all about it."

"I don't believe you." No, damn it! That wasn't what I should have said. I should have said...

"Honest. Feel for yourself. Nothing but skin under this li'l ol' dress. Aren't you going to feel?"

"No! You're trying to trick me, but it's no good, kid. Steel-will Loring they used to call me in the old days." I felt strong and sure of myself now.

"So you think I'm lying, do you? Well, we can't have that." With a jerk, she threw my towel to the floor and eased her hips as far forward as they would go. "Well?"

"Aarrgh!"

"Hmmm?"

"Aarrgh!"

"All right, if you insist." And so it passed, that day imploded into night and whippoorwills ricocheted off scintillating rose-hued moondrops bursting into thunderous roaring waves of amber-flowered nectar-glowing peace. What did you expect after two days of abstinence?

Much later, I was jumping lightly through the air and nearly caught my foot between the cement wharf and the side of the ferryboat that had taken me to Goree. I was glad the dark forces of resistentialism had missed. It was my favorite foot.

Resistentialism, for all you clods, is the theory that matter is not inert, but sentient. And it doesn't like man, particularly. Have you ever walked across a rug and tripped when there was nothing to trip over? Or have you ever been working under a car, without any doubt of where you are, and nevertheless slam your head up against the drive shaft? Or how about that third step that squeaks *just* when it shouldn't? That's resistentialism. Some things don't like us.

Anyway, I gathered up my Positive Mental Attitude and made my way through the crowd of tourists in their absurd costumes, and screaming, sticky schoolkids on vacation. Goree Island was outstanding today. It was amazing that after hundreds of years it could still remind one of Portugal. As I walked along the wharf I glanced at the young boys treading water in front of the ferry. They were chattering excitedly and diving for coins in the clear water. I would like to have been right in there with them. Not for the coins.

The sun was beating down hard and bright and I was anxious to sit in the shade with a cold drink. Across the tiny harbor I could see Demba's launch. Demba himself would be waiting for me at the Hotel *Espadon* on the other side of the island. At the end of the wharf I paused to admire some of the bikini-clad wonders stretched out on Goree's mini-beach, then turned left and ambled over the sand past the tired police station, through the welcome shade of a baobab tree (did you know the bark of the baobab tree can be used for rope, the leaves for soup, the fruit for a lemon substitute, the seeds for a type of coffee, and the hollow interior for a tomb? I didn't think so.) and into the hotel. Demba was sitting at a small table on the terrace. Behind him the white skyline of Dakar two miles away thrust itself into the enveloping arms of the deep, blue-green sea. It made a nice effect.

I sat down and ordered Stork beer, a local variety, but better than most of the imported stuff to my taste. "Well, Demba, I'm waiting to find out who wants to send me into the spirit world."

"You'll have to go on waiting, my friend. Gomez didn't reveal much more at my office than he did at the apartment. Two days ago, make that three, Gomez was approached by a blond sailor who offered to pay him for getting you killed, or at least badly injured. If you were killed or maimed, the sailor said he would know and Gomez would be paid at the *Taverne du Port* the same night. If you weren't, the sailor wouldn't show. A very neat arrangement."

"How much was he going to pay?"

"Fifty thousand francs."

"Two hundred dollars? That's all I'm worth on the open market?"

"At least at that price you'll only get amateurs."

"The trouble with amateurs is they're too messy. A clean, quick kill by a pro would be a lot better."

"I can arrange it if you're really interested."

"Thanks anyway. Hell, Demba, you know what I mean. This shakes me up."

"You've been in danger of being killed before, plenty of times."

"Sure, but I always knew why. That's the difference. If I know why someone wants to kill me I can be on my guard and accept the situation. Since I don't know why, I can't accept it. Therefore I stand a better chance of getting killed. And to be honest, that scares me." If all this psychology is too much for you, hang on. It's almost over.

"I'll see about getting you a bodyguard."

"I may need two. Darla's in town."

Demba looked surprised, then laid a huge hand on my arm. "That, my friend, is a real problem."

"That's not all, ol' buddy. Rokhaya's with her."

He choked on his coke. "That's a catastrophe! When did you see them?"

"I only saw Darla, but they're here together, 'on vacation.' We're having dinner with them."

"Sometimes you do the craziest things." Demba looked around the terrace, which was beginning to fill up with tourists. "Let's finish this up at the fort."

We paid the tab and walked out of the hotel. As we turned into a narrow street that led up the island's single hill to the old fort, I noticed an African who had been lazily leaning against a tree opposite the hotel entrance jump up and run out of sight down another street. My mind registered that as odd, but didn't linger on it. Demba and I marched in silence on the worn stones past the decrepit Catholic church and up the old carriage path. Near the top we climbed a flight of crumbling stairs under a faded exhortation, "HONNEUR ET PATRIE," and stepped onto a grassy plateau riddled with trenches, tunnels, and gun emplacements. All that was left of the thousands of men who had fought and died here through the centuries. Somebody would build a hotel there soon. We picked out an empty gun emplacement overlooking the port and began to talk.

"Tell me more about Darla and Rokhaya."

"What's to tell? They're on vacation and just want to have a good time. They picked us because we're the best lovers on the whole West African coast."

"Do you believe that?"

"Of course! Nobody can screw the way I do." Demba heaved a big sigh. "All right," I conceded, "I don't believe they're here on vacation anymore than you do. We both know they only play for the highest stakes. Why should they drop in now, when the only thing that's happening is the Mauritania thing? There has to be a connection, but I'm damned if I can think of one. I've been to Aoudaghost and I've read what the French have found there. Nothing worth ten thousand dollars and nothing worth luring Darla and Rocky out from under their respective rocks. I don't know. Maybe they do just want to ball for old time's sake."

"If it's for old time's sake, I'd rather strangle them.

"One smile from Rocky and you'll be tame as a puppy and you know it."

Demba looked at me with a sideways smirk. "And I suppose you are quite immune to the wicked charms of Darla?"

"I," said I, blithely ignoring the morning's events as well as several events in the past, "am capable of controlling my passion under any circumstances."

"Ho, ho."

"That was a snide remark."

"No, I beg your pardon. Those were two snide remarks. Ho and ho. Let me add a few more for the record. Ho, ho, ho."

"Let's change the subject. Where do you want to go for dinner?"

"That's not changing the subject, it's reducing it to an absurdity. You don't fight fire by jumping in the middle of it."

"How else are we going to find out what they're up to?"

"You won't find out till Darla throws you off another bridge."

"I'm afraid she won't get the chance. I'm going to Mauritania and leave the whole little mystery in your lap."

"You're not going anywhere, *toubab*." That wasn't Demba. It was a husky, grinning African who suddenly appeared at one of the entrances to the emplacement. He had somebody behind him and two more appeared at the other entrance. They all had nice sharp knives held at the ready.

Demba addressed them in Wolof. "Peace be with you."

The big one who spoke first answered him. "And

with you, peace. We don't have any quarrel with you, brother. Just with the *toubab*. He has to be cut up a little for his own good. You'll be safer on the other side of the hill." He moved aside a bit to let Demba pass through.

"The *toubab* is my brother. Whatever he suffers, so do I."

"It's your blood." He signaled to the others to move in and during that brief span of inattention I acted.

"YAAAAAAHHH!" The shout froze them long enough for me to bound between them, leap onto the four foot wall of the emplacement, and jump into space. I landed ten feet down, rolled, and dropped into a manhole that sucked air into the tunnels. Without waiting for my eyes to adjust to the darkness I felt for the wall I knew was there and guided myself a few feet along to a small room that was formerly used for storing ammunition. Less than a minute had passed and I expected the whole army to come after me any second.

I know what you're thinking. What a lousy coward to leave his friend up there against all those guys. Have you ever tried to fight four knives with your fingernails? I don't usually carry a gun, and I don't go around with superbombs hidden in my watch or shirt buttons that give off poison gas. Oh, I have a pipe tool with a knife blade on it, but if you think I'd face them with that, you're an idiot. Why didn't I use savotte and kick all their teeth in? Sorry, never studied it. I know enough karate to kill someone if I have to, but I never met the man who could use it on four armed men at once. Can't you just see it? My fingers shoot out with deadly accuracy for the throat of one man while his partner reaches over with his knife and WHAP! no fingers. No thank you. Besides, they were after me, not Demba. They probably all chased after me when I escaped and left him alone. Maybe that's an afterthought, but it's comforting.

I heard a distant shout, a close rustling sound. Acid rock had nearly ruined my ears, but I could still make out what sounded like feet shuffling through the litter on the floor of the main tunnel. There were no lights at all down here and I knew whoever it was couldn't see me by glomming the room. On the other hand, there was just enough light in the main tunnel to let me pick out his white shirt as he tippie-toed past my doorway. Now came the big choice. Should I let him go on by and sit there nice and safe, or should I rush out and wrestle with him before his buddies arrived? But what if his buddies were already on their way?

It didn't really matter. While my reason was sorting this out, my body had taken the initiative and charged the enemy with a neat flying tackle that took both of us sliding across the cruddy deck with my nose rubbing concrete all the way. Automatic reactions can be dangerous as hell. He landed on top, naturally, and I panicked, thinking of that beautiful skin of mine about to be sliced by an unsterilized knife. With a convulsive kick I threw him off and tried to get to my feet. Instantly I felt a burning pain in my left calf and I knew he'd connected with the knife. As I fell back down I realized the bastard had just ruined my new Pierre Cardin slacks. He was on me in a second. Infinite Intelligence guided my fingers to the wrist of his knife hand, but his other one gripped my former free hand and held it flat to the deck. Are you with me?

This cat must have worked out regularly, 'cause he was squeezing my wrist so hard my fingers were getting numb. I could tell I'd been exercising the wrong muscles lately. I let one arm go limp and concentrated all my strength on holding that knife back. Unfortunately, from my point of view he was holding it the wrong way, with the blade toward his thumb. My grip was okay, but his arm was sweaty and bit by bit my hand slid in the direction of his elbow. Finally, I could feel the point of the knife against my ribs. He was breathing hard, his mouth open, and I could see his teeth shining in the darkness. There's only one thing to do in such a situation. Cheat. I hacked up the biggest oyster I could find and spat it right between his *machoires* (you ignos who don't speak French can find that on page 430 of Larousse's French-English Dictionary, 1960 edition).

There may be a man alive who can take that without flinching, but this wasn't one of them. His flinch let me break loose with my limp hand and whap him in the aqueduct. While he gurgled I heaved him off and kicked him in the groin for good measure. My adrenalin had gone to my head and for a second or two I wanted to jump up and down on him with both feet. With a terrible effort I left him groveling in the filth and dashed into the blinding blackness of a side tunnel, tripped over a plank, and landed flat out in something soft, squishy, and smelly. Yecch!

An instant later, I heard another one of the hunters coming down the main tunnel from the opposite direction. I scrambled around and grabbed hold of the plank, which I found I could lift. I edged up to the entrance of my hideout. Sweat was burning my eyes, crap was dribbling down my chest, and I tried desperately to convince myself that the other guy couldn't hear my wheezy breathing. As soon as I saw his shadowy figure cross in front of me I lunged. Thrack! I got him in the hip and he went down, yelling like a wounded lion. Like a lion, he tried to get up again and I pounced on him, using his slight momentum to grab him by the seat of his pants and his shirt and run him with all my might into the nearest wall. Blam! Off he bounced, hardly the worse for all my work since the sonofabitch had protected himself with his arms. He hadn't even let go of his knife. He got up cursing and headed for me with really evil intent. Suddenly I remembered the trick from early boyhood that I used whenever the big guys tried to pick on me. I ran. Turned tail and scooted right back down that side tunnel as fast as I could go. It was a silly thing to do.

The tunnel ended in a blank wall after about twenty yards. I scrunched down in what seemed to be the blackest corner and tried to mute my gasps. I got ready to lash out at crotch level with my heel and strained ears for the slightest sound. A cockroach scratched his way across my arm. Somewhere close a rat-like rustle started and stopped, restarted and stopped again. Other than that there was only my breathing. For a terrifying second I thought I might be drowning out the sound of his approach. I opened my mouth wide to lessen the noise. Still nothing. Maybe he was tying his shoelace. An itch came to life on my left leg and worked its way steadily up to my nose. I tried to concentrate on the clear and present danger, but the itch began to draw all my attention. A fierce desire welled up in me for a cool shower and a hot woman. And here I was waiting to die, full of shit and itch. I wanted to cry. Poor me. I honestly think tears came to my eyes. Then suddenly a light flashed on me and I yelped in panic. Every muscle tensed in anticipation of the ripping, slashing blade that was going to tear the flesh from my bones.

"Oh, I'm sorry. I thought you were someone I knew."

Demba! Gratitude almost reduced me to a blubbering idiot. I kept myself from kissing his feet and slowly, achingly rose to my own. "It's a good thing you spoke. I might have torn you to bits without thinking."

He turned the penlight upward to show his mug. He grinned ghastily. "Yeah, boy, I sure am lucky."

We went out into the light. There was no sign of our assailants. I was too tired to ask about it just yet and besides, the brilliant sunshine gave me a brilliant headache. I couldn't go down to the dock looking and smelling like a human sewer, so we made our way to the seaward cliff and took a path down to the water. There I stripped to my skivvies and bathed in a rocky pool while Demba related his end of the adventure. After my gazelle-like leap into space, the leader of the pack left one guy to guard Demba and took the rest after me. Naturally, that was a mistake. Demba disarmed his guard with no sweat and put him out with a karate chop. Peering over the wall, he saw no one but another stud standing over the manhole. Demba gently jumped on his back and used the man's own knife to pry out some choice bits of info. Then he turned the stud's lights out and dumped him headfirst into the hole, following feetfirst after. He found my nemesis hesitating before the side tunnel, and as you all know, he who hesitates is lost, Demba quietly disposed of him and dragged all three bodies into the storage room where I had first hidden. Then he came into the tunnel to tell me that all the bad men were gone away and I could come out now.

At the last bit I came out of the water sputtering, but he was laughing, and a moment later so was I.

After rinsing and redonning my dacron bush suit we headed back to the port. The sun would dry it in just a few minutes. On the way, Demba related his knife-gotten gains. The setup was almost the same. Apparently the same blond swabbie had recommenced recruiting and he hadn't wasted any time doing it. This time he had picked up some longshoremen short on cash. I was obviously being tailed and the memory had pried one other bit of info out of his unwilling informer. The object of the attack was to either kill me or cut me up so badly I would have to be hospitalized. In other words, immobilized. In even other words, maybe someone was trying to keep me from going to Mauritania.

On reaching what passes for downtown Goree, Demba stopped briefly at the police station and minutes later three happy cops went dashing up the hill. You can't imagine how dull life gets on Goree.

We went back to the mainland on Demba's launch, made arrangements for two of his men to tail me closely until I left for Aoudaghost, and decided on where to take our deadly dates for dinner. Demba was both reluctant and impatient. Rokhaya had a wild effect on him. It's a pity how some men have a weakness for women.

4/M'Bao

While waiting for the arrival of the dangerous duo, I treated myself to a *Ricard* (a brand of *pastis,* if you're curious) and Demba sipped on his ever-present Coke. The girls had promised to meet us at eight and it was now quarter to nine. We were sitting in the tiny lounge of the Lagon, one of the finest restaurants in Dakar. It's really just a dock jutting out into a small bay and all fancied up with nautical decorations, but the food it outtasight. Also, the surf beneath your feet and the stars overhead give it a touch of glamour that warms even my jaded heart.

Ordinarily, a woman (or two, in this case) being late for an engagement wouldn't be anything to get too upset about, but Demba and I couldn't help imagining Demba and Rocky spending the time putting a bomb in our car or mining the entrance to our apartments. What nonsense, you say? Dear, naive reader, let me give you some historical perspective.

Let me begin with Darla, whom you've met. Ms. Darla Moore (the first surname under which I met her) was at this time somewhere around twenty-five years old and possibly of American origin, though she had passed for French, Hungarian, Argentinian, and half a dozen others. Darla belongs to an organization called—get this—the Lorelei. Melodramatic, what? In the mythic literature, the lorelei were wicked females who lured men to their doom. Does the picture begin to take on a semblance of clarity? Darla's happy group specializes in providing very highly trained female agents to governments and commercial interests all over the world for a multitude of nefarious deeds. No one knows how the girls are recruited, but they are picked up early and trained to perfection as killers, lovers, spies, and what have you. As I understand it, all the girls have to major in male psychology, the practice of which they have raised to the status of an art. The success of the Lorelei depends a lot on their secrecy, and for all I know they have a master plan to conquer the world. What little I do know was gleaned arduously over a period of years in both favorable and unfavorable circumstances. Darla, for one, I know to be absolutely ruthless. The only reason she didn't kill me in Ghana was because she didn't have orders to.

Rocky is of the same breed, but slightly more is known about her. She was born Rokhaya Fall, a

Senegalese. At the age of fifteen she went to France as a domestic for the family of a French businessman. After getting knocked up, presumbly by her boss, she disappeared, only to turn up some eight years later on a diamond-smuggling caper, during which she broke Demba's heart into teeny weeny bits. She broke another man's back at the same time.

So Demba and I were worried. They had to be here on business, and since they had sought us out we were either unwilling partners or victims.

"Here they come." We stood. I almost applauded. Deadly and ruthless they might be, but they were exciting females, nonetheless. Rocky wore a floor-length indigo *boubou* of African cloth that floated sensuously around her as she descended the steps to the lounge. Her hair was done up in a couple dozen miniature braids that hung down around her head and framed her delicate features. Darla, in keeping with her personality, was more flamboyant. Her dress also swept her ankles, but it clung to her body like it was in love with her. It was white with gold embroidery and was slit up to the top of one leg. A golden garter peeked out teasingly as she walked. Every eye in the place was on them and in our egotistic male way, Demba and I couldn't help preening ourselves a little when they came up to us.

Amenities over, I signaled the owner, who led us to the lobster tank to choose our unlucky main courses. Except for me, that is. Ever since I learned that lobsters scream with pain when thrown into the boiling pot I prefer to eat something else. Squeamish? Maybe. Some people won't eat rats and lizards. Tonight, though, I settled for one of the house specialties. *Steak au poivre,* thick, tender beef smothered in a creamy pepper sauce. Yum! I must be hungry. Let's get back to the story.

"Where have you been, Rocky?" asked Demba. "It's been a long time since you've passed through."

"Oh, I've been in the Far East, studying history."

"Or making it?" I suggested. She merely smiled.

Conversation during dinner dealt mostly with inanities. The subject of business came up over cognac.

Darla began in her roundabout way. "Why don't we all fly out to the Canaries this weekend? We could rent a two-bedroom villa, dance all night and make love all day."

"Sounds great," I said. "Demba and I know a couple of girls we can bring along, but what are you going to do?"

Rocky put her hand on Demba's. "I'm sure Demba would prefer the present company, wouldn't you?" If Rocky's libido could be seen as a tangible object, it would have been in the shape of a thick noose. And Demba would have put it on with his own hands. As it was, he didn't answer. He just drooled.

I recognized the leg nudging me under the table as being Darla's. She turned her wicked smile number one on full power. "It would be worthwhile, Lee. I've learned some new tricks since the last time."

I laughed. "I'll bet you have. But I have to disappoint you. I have a date to go skiing in Pakistan this weekend."

"Somehow I don't believe you."

"That's okay. Somehow I don't believe you're here on vacation."

"Why Lee," Rocky cooed, "how can you be so suspicious? Here we are just dying to get you two in the sack and you keep looking for an ulterior motive. You believe us, don't you, Demba?"

Demba looked at me. There was a glaze over his eyes. "Lee, it's possible..."

"This game has gone far enough! Demba, get the stars out of your eyes and drag your mind away from Rocky's body. She must have put something in your drink." It was harsh on a friend, but Demba was getting ridiculous. I signaled the waiter for refills. Turning back to the girls, I said, "Now, let's play it straight. You two are here on business, but I don't know what kind, yet. Whoever gave you the script for the sexpot gambit was a lousy writer. We know each other well enough not to insult each other's intelligence. I'll start the plain talk by saying that there have been two attempts on my life in the past two days and I think you two are involved. Since they weren't successful, somebody sent you here to stop me from doing whatever I'm planning to do. So what's your side?"

My outburst didn't ruffle them. They didn't even exchange glances. All I noticed was that Darla narrowed her eyes a little before she spoke. "Your reasoning is good, but your facts are wrong. We only learned about the attacks on your life today. Yes, we were sent to stop you from going to Mauritania tomorrow by any means of our choice. Failing the Canary ploy, which I didn't think would work, we'd have found something else short of killing you, if possible. If not, well, there are high stakes involved."

When Darla decided to be frank she didn't fool around. "What do you know about the Mauritania trip?"

Rocky answered. "That you've been hired to take two archeologists to Aoudaghost. That somebody doesn't want two archeologists poking around there. That somebody particularly doesn't want *you* poking around there. And that if you are stopped the whole trip will have to be called off. As for the attempts on your life, we don't know if that was our employer or not."

By now Demba had loosened Rocky's noose enough to make sense again. "Do you know anything about the two archeologists?"

"Nothing. That wasn't covered in our instructions. Our assignment was to stop Lee from taking the trip. I am curious to know what's so important up there, though."

Darla chuckled. "Unfortunately, curiosity pays a poor rate of return. All we're being paid to do is carry out our assignment." She was still smiling.

I decided to assert my masculinity. "I fully intend to go to Mauritania tomorrow."

"We fully intend to stop you."

It was Demba's turn to laugh. "In chess, that's called a stalemate. Unless you've got a really tricky move planned, Lee."

"The only thing I have planned right now is a good night's sleep." I called for the bill. It was true that I didn't have anything planned, but I was thinking about hiring twenty-five guards to escort me to the airport.

"Lee, let's not end the evening on a bitter note." Darla took my arm "We can spend the rest of the night together and forget about the trip till tomorrow."

"Not on your life," I said as I headed out. "I see through your plan. You want to wear me out so I won't even be able to get up in the morning." Beneath the laughter, we all knew that war had been declared. Me against superwoman. Demba would help any way he could, of course, but I was the target.

On reaching the cars we found an unpleasant surprise. All four tires on the car Darla and Rocky had rented were flat.

"What kind of trick is this?" I asked. "A sneaky way to get a ride in my car so you can poke a knife in my ribs or something?"

"Goddamn you and your twisted mind! We didn't do this! If Rocky and I had wanted to stop you here we'd have planted a bomb in your car."

Demba and I did exchange glances. However, no bombs were found after a thorough inspection. "It could have been a prank," he said. I gave him a withering, but friendly, look. "Then again, maybe someone wants us all together." Without another word he rushed back down to the restaurant. In less than five minutes he was back. "I called my office. One of the men is bringing another car over. Shall we split up or just leave your car here, Lee?"

"We'll split up. Darla and I will take my car and

you follow with Rocky in the other. If we meet with any trouble you can act as reinforcements." I also wanted to split up the two girls. I still wasn't sure this wasn't their doing. As it turned out it was one of my dumber decisions.

Demba's man arrived with the car a few minutes later. I took the lead in my Citroen DS and headed downtown. I wanted to get the girls to the N'Gor Hotel so I could be free to make my own arrangements for getting to Mauritania. They were acting so sure about stopping me that I was sure the action had to take place either on the way to the hotel or, more in keeping with Darla's dramatic flair, the next morning just before the plane was due to take off. I didn't think Darla would try anything before we got to the hotel, not without Rocky and not while we were in the car. Besides, no one had offered to pay me for not going to Mauritania yet. The flat tire bit was confusing. It wasn't Darla's style. There was an off chance that a third party wanted me out of the way, but if so, why try to get all of us together? My mind felt like it was full of cobwebs.

There were two routes to N'Gor from the city. One was the Corniche, along the ocean. It had quite a number of possible ambush sites. The other route led along a straight five kilometer freeway to a new residential section called *Patte d'Oie* (Goosefoot, in English. French is *so* much more poetic). From there another highway led to the airport along the north side of the peninsula. I chose the latter way because it allowed for greater speed.

Demba was right behind me until we got to the

entrance of the freeway. After that I couldn't see his lights in the rear-view mirror. What the hell had happened? At the *Patte d'Oie* intersection there was a car parked off the road. I was sure I saw a man leaning against it with something about the size of a transistor radio next to his ear as we turned left for N'Gor. I cursed myself for the egotism that made me have my Citroen painted a bright metallic blue.

"Your friends seem to have us spotted. What's next?"

Darla called me an unfathered child and went on, "Since when did I ever need any help?"

There was no time for conversation. The residential section was behind us and there was nothing but sand dunes on either side of us. Just ahead two Land Rovers were parked on opposite sides of the road, facing in our direction. About five hundred yards further, two small trucks were parked in the same way. As we passed the Land Rovers they started up after us. Guessing the next move, I quickly geared down. I was right. The trucks turned into the road to block our path and twenty guys or so leaped out to greet us. I screeched to a halt within fifty yards of them and rammed the gear shift into reverse. We whined away to the rear and I was hoping the two drivers of the Land Rovers would be too surprised to act logically.

My personal gods were still with me. Instead of knocking me silly with a sideswipe, both of them split for the edge of the road. Sometimes working against amateurs has its advantages. Once past them, I turned around and set out lickety-split toward Goosefoot. The Rover is a good vehicle, but it has a wide turning radius and a low top speed. No more problem from them.

Back at the intersection, I decided not to slow down for the turn, but kept going straight down the road to Rufisque, a not-too-distant hamlet. The road was fairly straight and I could keep up my high speed. Traffic, as you may have guessed already, was very light. I was beginning to feel I had gotten away once again when two headlights began closing up on us. That car was *fast*. In Rufisque I would have to slow down, and that wouldn't do me any good. So I tortured my poor brakes once more and took a sharp right on a dirt road to M'Bao beach. On that deserted strand we would have our showdown.

On the beach, I whipped my car around in a wide circle and stopped. The spotter was right behind us. Darla and I hopped out, me armed with an eight-inch knife I keep under the seat for emergencies. The adversaries were also out and at the ready. Two were Africans, holding one tire iron each. The third (I thanked somebody there were only three) had a knife.

You'll have to excuse me for breaking the narrative at this point, but I can practically hear the snide remarks of some of the less-traveled readers. "What's with all the knives and clubs? Why doesn't anybody have a gun?" Well, I'll tell you. The governments in Africa are *very* touchy about civilians toting guns around. A revolution is always just around the corner and anyone who is not a member of the police or the military and who is caught with a gun is immediately suspected of anti-government activities. Permits are issued sparingly for hunting rifles, but hand-guns are generally a no-no. Wherever there has been a good-sized revolution or civil war, however, you'll be more apt to find them.

Now, back to the story. As you recall, the third guy to step out of the other car had a knife. He also had blond hair and a moustache. No doubt the sailor boy who was causing all the trouble. He gestured towards me. "Get him! I'll take care of the girl." Those were the last words he ever spoke.

The Africans circled to each side of me. I couldn't fight both at once with a knife, so I got rid of it by throwing it away. Right in the belly of the cat on my left. A second later I was grabbing the iron from his hand as he fell. I twisted around to meet the attack of the other one, but not quite quickly enough. He got me on the left shoulder with a blow that made my teeth curl. I was down and he was up and I desperately wanted to change that arrangement. Whang! Our irons met in strike and parry. For a moment I felt like I was a teenager again on the streets of Detroit. He raised his club to strike at me again, but instead of trying to block the blow I cracked him on the kneecap. I was still hit on the head, but not nearly as hard as I might have been. He was down and howling, so I crawled over and put him out of his misery. The whole affair didn't take more than two or three minutes. It's only in the movies that a serious fight goes on and on.

Head aching and shoulder throbbing with pain, I looked around for Darla. She was sitting on the stretched out blond, looking through his wallet. "Is he dead?"

She looked up and smiled. "Yes, I'm afraid I crushed his windpipe. Men are so fragile."

The daughters of Lilith are still among us, I thought. "Anything in the wallet?"

"Oh, things and stuff. A seaman's card, a couple of nasty pictures, a receipt from the Hotel de Paris, and lots of dollars and francs." She put the money in her bra and stood up.

"I'll see if I can have his room searched. What was his name?"

"I doubt if you'll find anything in his room. And the name on the card isn't his. At least it's not the one he had when I last met him. His name then was Hans Meitner, supposedly a Swiss citizen. This does change things."

"How about telling me what and why?"

She came over and touched my bloody head, making me wince. "First, let's take care of your bruises. Then I'll tell you."

We took both cars and drove to a nearby Catholic mission. The good fathers were more than helpful. They not only patched me up, but insisted we have some of their best mass wine before we left. I told them my brakes had locked to explain my bruises, and then asked them if I could leave the car there for someone to pick it up the next day. They agreed readily and another problem was solved.

Darla and I took the other car back to Dakar and on the way she let out just a little bit more info.

"Meitner did dirty little jobs in Europe for whoever would pay him. There were rumors that he had been in the Nazi SS, but nearly every German has to cope with that. He was very good at his work, a real expert at covering up his traces and no less at carrying out his assignments. I'm surprised he didn't try to take care of you himself instead of using the local amateurs. Maybe he was slowing down, or felt he was too conspicuous here. Or maybe he didn't think too highly of you."

"Haven't I been wounded enough tonight? Do you know who he was working for last?"

"No, it's been a couple of years since I've heard of him. He was the hit man for a smuggling feud then. Oh, well, I wouldn't worry about it."

I nearly ran the car off the road. "You wouldn't worry about it!" I blew up. "Of course you wouldn't worry about it, no one's trying to end *your* breathing!"

She laughed, a full-throated and relaxed sound. "You get so carried away sometimes. Meitner's dead, so it's okay now, li'l fella. I'll protect you."

It was night or she would have seen my tan turn magenta. Sure, she was goading me—and succeeding in getting my blood to boil—but I do not even like to have it intimated that I am under the protection of the female of the species. Not even a protectress as obviously competent as Darla. Any of you amateur psychologists who think that that reveals a basic insecurity in my make-up are totally wrong. It's simply chauvinism. At any rate, it was also time to remember that this woman had made a contract to stop me from going about my appointed rounds by any means possible and necessary. With that thought I found my hackles rising and my right arm tensing to block off any potential strikes she might make from her side. "Thank you for taking care of Meitner," I said, carefully controlling my voice so as to leave it devoid of all clues to my preparedness.

A chuckle. "It'll be a bit difficult to fight me off as long as you have to keep one hand on the wheel. Your right hand is too high to be effective against a kidney chop and your arm is too tense. Relax it a little and you'll increase your speed." She touched my shoulder and I jumped. She touched my thigh and I jumped again. She touched my...

"Now cut that out! You're my declared enemy. So don't give me advice on how to defend myself and lay off my private parts."

"Private parts?" She howled. "Lee, your parts haven't been private since you came out of the womb. If they were displayed at the Louvre every third woman passing by would recognize them without looking at the plaque."

"Please!" I exclaimed, torn between a rush of ego and wondering where the rest of me would be. "Let's knock off the cute talk and remember who and where we are. I've been offered a certain sum of money to take two innocents to a place where your boss and others don't want me to go. I'm a reasonable man. Make me a good counter-offer and maybe I'll quietly stay here."

"Put me down as doubting the innocence of both the archeologists. The woman reminds me of a cobra. As for a counter-offer, you refused my bod' so how about if I break both your legs?"

"Miss Benedetti is obviously as pure as ...as...well, anyway, what I had in mind was money, not violence." By now we had pulled up to the front of the N'Gor Hotel. "Don't I get an easy out?"

"I was told to detain you for at least four weeks. No one authorized any payments, so I have to choose less expensive methods. Still, Meitner's presence might have changed things. I'll have to call Circe and let you know. Want to wait?" She smiled fetchingly. "In my room?" She smiled lecherously.

Circe was Lorelei HQ. Employment for Darla and her gang was always filtered through Circe for their protection. The girls never had any direct contact with the clients. This allowed the organization a lot of leeway for carrying out assignments. "Thanks, I'm tempted beyond belief, but I just want to go home and rest my weary head and..."

"I'll take care of your head."

"Give up, woman, for crying out loud!" Taking my life in my hands, I reached over and opened the door. "Out. We'll have our showdown in the morning." She removed herself and stood on the curb.

"Lee." Her voice was low and serious. "I like you more than most men, but if I decide to stop you from going to Mauritania you won't be going. If it has to be done the rough way, then that's the way it'll be done. You understand?"

I gave her my most forgiving smile. "Sure thing, baby. See you at the airport." She was looking at me skeptically as I drove off.

The Citroen roared back into town. With me at the wheel, of course. I mean, it didn't go all by itself because... oh, forget it. A wild idea had flashed in my brain and I was going to carry it out before I had a chance to think about it. If I thought about it too much Darla might pick it up on the telepathic airwaves and I didn't want to take that chance. First stop was at the tiny Hotel de la Place where I used the telephone to try and raise Demba. No luck. I wasted a few curse words on Rocky. By keeping him out of contact with me they were cutting down my efficiency, as they well knew. Next I tried Sami. No answer there, either. Now, that was wrong! Sami or one of his sons was always available. I didn't have time to speculate, so I called Aletha. Another blank. Little toadstools of panic sprouted in my stomach. They were blocking off my best resources. So I went radical and switched to Plan Z.

Plan Z was desperation time. There were at least a hundred people I could have contacted, from diplomats, to government officials, to businessmen, to art traders, laborers and not a few girlfriends, but the word that Loring was running from something would have spread like tahine sauce from any of them. And that wouldn't be any good for either my rep or my health. It had to be Plan Z.

I've done one hell of a lot of strange things in my life. Yet, the number one was when I did a stint of training as a sorcerer, or *fetisheur,* as it is called in this part of the world. My reasoning at the time was that it would be a good way to get deeper insight into the meaning of the various art objects in which I dealt. I got the insight. I also got much more than I expected. To be truthful, it frightened me out of my ever-loving wits! I learned that there are incredibly different ways of looking at the world, ways that produce results that are absolutely impossible by any normal standards. Yet, they work. Oh, yes, they work. It is almost as if there are two different worlds co-existing in the same space on this planet. To use an inadequate analogy; in one world—the one most of us are brought up in—everything is black and white, while in the other it is a kaleidoscope of color. It really can't be explained. We don't have the right words. The point is that there are some people—the true *fetisheurs*—who can slip easily in and out of both of them and are comfortable in either. My training, bought at a price I'd not care to mention, was short and sketchy, but I'd had a glimpse of the rainbow. Its beauty and strangeness was too much for me to handle, and so I ran back to "normality" as fast as I could skedaddle. Still, the ones who trained me now considered me a sort of low-grade initiate (a sorcerer's apprentice?) and as far as they were concerned it was a life-time commitment. Since that first experience so many years ago I had only sought their help once. The results of that help, though effective, were enough to make me swear never to do it again. And here I was. I may not be consistent about promises, but I am consistent about trying to save my skin. Plan Z was to contact my *okora,* a kind of sorcerer-advisor, for assistance. I hadn't even seen him in four years, but I knew how to get in touch with him.

I drove the Citroen to a purely African quarter of Dakar, a place with dirt streets and crowded hovels made of rattan, old boards and occasional galvanized sheeting. This particular section was not a safe place for "Europeans" to be at night. I was out of my territory and very edgy. There were no street lights, just a few kerosene lanterns hung here and there. A noisy dance was being held down one alley I passed. Half-dressed children dashed in front of the car as I slowly moved along. It would be instantly deadly to risk the slightest accident in this place. Finally, I parked outside a tattered car, disembarked and went in.

It was lit with one lantern swinging precariously from an overhead rafter. I could make out four or five figures in the semi-darkness drinking *Stork*. They were big men. This was a hangout for the rough trade and just the color of my skin could spark off a rumble. In addition, the atmosphere was heavy with fumes of *"l'herbe qui tue"* (the herb that kills), the local journalistic phrase for marijuana.

At my entrance the boisterous talking gave way to a nasty silence. Then a fella who was much too large for my taste heaved himself up in front of me. "Salaam alek," I said with a smile. He replied by taking a butcher knife out of his belt and wiping it on his arm while just staring with decidedly unfriendly eyes. Softly, trying not to make any sudden facial movements, I said, "Baba N'Dow?" His reaction was immediate. His eyes grew wide with fear and he swiftly returned to his seat and faced away from me. I noticed that all the others turned away, too. Baba N'Dow was the name of my *okora*. Obviously, he was well-known.

"Viens!" A tiny voice caused me to turn back to the doorway. A small boy, not more than eight or nine, was beckoning for me to follow him. This was the kind of thing that always unnerved me. How did he know I was coming? I didn't feel like thinking

about it too much, so I just followed the boy through a warren of huts until we came to one that looked like all the others. The boy motioned me to go inside. I pushed aside the cloth covering the doorway and entered. My *okora* was sitting there as if he were dozing. He wore a wool knit cap similar to the ones worn by many of the Moslems in West Africa. He had on a once-white robe that left his scrawny chest bare and around his neck on a leather cord hung a squarish gold fetish, a box containing dark secrets. By the way, the word "fetish," as used in this area, can mean anything from an amulet to a full-sized mask or statue, as long as it has been charged with the power of a sorcerer. No lantern here. The dregs of a candle sputtered in a dish on his right, apparently ready to go out at any moment. The damn thing kept sputtering the whole half hour I was there.

I sat down cross-legged in front of him. "Salaam alek. Diam reck," I greeted him. He paid no more attention to me than if I were a fly. I couldn't tell if he were really sleeping or not, so I went on as if he weren't. I told him of the whole affair up to the present, all about the archeologists, the attempts on my life, and the arrival of Rocky and Darla. Then I said, "I need your help." No response. I plunged ahead. "I want to go to Kaolack and take a private plane from there to Tamchakett in Mauritania. I want to leave immediately. I need a change of clothes and some money because I can't risk going back to my place or trying to see my friends. This is all I want." It was the idea of going to Kaolack, a two-hour drive to the south, that had come to me as I let Darla off. There was no way she or anyone else could know what I had in mind if I left right away. Providing I could get the plane, it was a foolproof way to get around her threat to stop me. Once in Mauritania I'd have to play it by ear. "I'll pay for everything when I return," I added lamely.

A long silence followed during which I almost fell asleep. At last I felt that if anything were going to happen my sitting around wasn't going to help. I started to get up when I was startled by a dry, crackling voice that gave me chills. Part of the reason was that it didn't look like his lips were moving at all, but the candlelight may have fooled me.

"Your life is like a flame in a wind. It may go out. It may not. While it burns you must eat the wood of the world, nevertheless. Soon the wind will grow much stronger. Sometimes..." He paused for ages. "Sometimes the wind can make a flame grow stronger." Another long pause. Then, "When you see the Face of God, eat its heart!"

I got the gist of the wind and flame idea, but the last phrase went right over my head. Before I could ask what he meant he reached out a thin hand and dropped a dirty leather sack into my lap. "Give this to the leader of the first camel train that you meet. Your training continues." And with that he picked up a kind of shawl, draped it over his head in a typical Moslem prayer attitude and began mumbling over his prayer beads. It was time for me to go.

How it was done I don't know, but when I emerged from the hut the boy led me to a black Peugeot. In it were the change of clothes I had requested and fifty thousand francs (about $200). As if he were reciting a memorized speech the boy told me where to meet the plane in Kaolack and said my own car would be taken care of and my friends notified. Then he disappeared into a nearby hut. The only thing left for me to do was get in the car and take off. As I sat in the driver's seat I felt some lumps under me. They were kola nuts, extremely bitter and chock full of natural caffeine. They were to keep me awake on the road to Kaolack. The bitterness would have been enough, but by the time I arrived at the airfield I felt like I wouldn't sleep for a week. However, the pilot could hardly keep his eyes open, so I forced some kola on him, too.

Like I said, "they" are spooky, but effective.

5/Tamchakett

Dawn over the desert. There's nothing quite like that change of color that creeps over the sand and rocks and brush, and the feeling of freshness that accompanies it. The early morning hours are delightfully cool and the sense of peace is overwhelming.

At the moment, I was still in the plane that had taken me from Kaolack. The engine roar was monotonous enough to enhance the sense of peace, rather than diminish it. We were flying at about two thousand feet and had already crossed the Senegal River that borders Mauritania and Senegal. From our height the land appeared as one vast, desolate plain, stretching to the whole horizon. No sign of life, yet down there were people being born, living, dying, and not even paying taxes. The desert certainly isn't crowded, but it isn't empty, either. It's almost impossible to go a hundred miles without running into somebody, unless they don't want to be seen.

Anyway, the place looks empty both from the air and the ground. Now, when I say empty, I don't mean a dune buggy's heaven of endless sand dunes. Sand dunes exist, but they form a very small part of the Saharan terrain. Most of the ground is rocky with scattered brush and occasional hills and mountain ranges. Very much like the American Southwest, in fact. What is bone dry now used to be green and lush, with flowing rivers. At that time there were thriving cities scattered about. Aoudaghost had been one of these, already fading when it was overrun by Morrocan invaders in the tenth or twelfth century. It was to this forgotten failure that we were heading, after landing at Tamchakett, the provincial headquarters.

At least, I hoped we were going to land there. There aren't many land marks in the desert and it's easy to get lost, even for an experienced pilot. To give you an idea of what we were trying to find, Tamchakett is an old French Foreign Legion fort surrounded by nothing. It is built from local rocks and mud and blends in beautifully with the countryside. Of course, there is no radio, no tower, no windsock, no runway; the "landing field" is a semi-flat plateau a quarter-mile from the fort. I was concerned enough to ask the pilot, an old Frenchman who flew in World War II, if he was sure of his heading.

"La ferme!" came the reply. *"Si tu es assez foutu de me faire venir dans ce foutu pays a cette heure foutue, tu peux t'emmerde!"*

Um, well, I don't think I'll translate that colorful passage. Get a French dictionary if you're that interested. Suffice to say that he recommended that I remain quiet and then expressed his unhappiness about the whole thing. Andre, the pilot, had been awakened before dawn, about the time I was finishing the talk with my *okora* (well, there are telephones, I told myself,) and he had to get out of a warm, snuggly and still occupied bed to ready his plane for some nut—*salopard* was the word I think he used—who wanted to go to Mauritania. I have no idea why he felt obliged, but although there was a lot of cursing, there was no hesitation. So I just crossed my fingers and toes and prayed a lot to four hundred thousand gods until I heard him shout.

"V'la!" He tipped the plane on edge and pointed. *"C'est la!"*

I'm not sure, but I think he seemed more relieved than I was. Looking down I could see the outlines of the fort with a few tents in the courtyard and around it. Outside the fort there were two Land Rovers and a truck. One of the Rovers was white with a blue star painted on top. That was mine, and as we circled to land it took off to meet us.

It felt like an eight point landing, but at least we didn't flip over and we didn't hit the other plane that was there. Andre brought the plane to a halt and I jumped out. *"Au revoir,"* I said with a friendly smile. "Thanks."

"T'en foutre!" he answered amiably, then

whipped his plane around and took off for the south. Nice guy. I'd have to bust his nose sometime. Ooooeeee! I forgot the sun. It was already hot enough to begin blistering my hair. In some parts of the world the sun beats down on you, but in the Sahara it attacks. The Land Rover wasn't here yet, so I tripped over to the other plane and stood under a wing. A quarter mile might not seem like much. In Mauritania, however, what passes for a road in most places would be unrecognizable elsewhere. The distance from Tamchakett to the nearest town is about two hundred miles and the last time I drove that it took eleven hours.

At last the Land Rover arrived and pulled up nearby. Out stepped Salif with his big grin, an armed militiaman from the fort (standard stuff), and ...Omigod! "No, no!," I cried, and dropped to the ground with my head in my hands. It was the scourge of sexland, that sinister sister of the slink set, Darla!

She came over, took me by the hands and brought me to my feet. "Lee, darling," she cooed, "you break down so easily. C'mon, the news is good. Let me tell you all about it." She turned back to the Rover and I couldn't help following. She had done herself up in short shorts of khaki with knee socks and shirt to match. The shirt, as you may have guessed, was mostly unbuttoned and tied in a knot at the level of her solar plexus. On her head she wore a French bush hat, like a soft Aussie-type. She was obviously showing off for someone for good reason, because first of all an outfit like that would drive the Moslem Moors up the wall, and second of all she was too good an expert at survival to wear an outfit like that for very long in the desert. Nevertheless, I followed the shorts to the vehicle, tearing my eyes away long enough to greet Salif and the soldier. The poor soldier didn't even see me, I don't think. To be fair, I barely saw him.

On the way to the fort Darla told me what had happened. "As soon as you left me at the hotel I called your friend Sami and told him that you were being held prisoner in one of the cabins on N'Gor Island and to get out there with all the help he could get. Then I called your secretary and told her the same thing. A lot of people seem to care about you, Lee."

I felt sorry for all the ones who did. "What voice did you use?" I grated.

"Oh, I think it was a close approximation of that silly ambassador's daughter you date once in a while. I thought you'd be trying to get in touch with either Sami or Aletha to pull some sneaky way of getting here, so I had to get them out of the way. Rocky was already taking care of Demba."

"Yes, I'd figured that."

"Mutually enjoyable, from what I heard. Anyway, I got in touch with some people I know and we covered your office, your boat and your various pads around town. They were even waiting on the road out to Dakar." She paused and gave me the full blast of her soft eyes. "How'd you do it, Lee? You didn't have much time and I already had people stationed at all the airports clear out to Kaolack. Want to satisfy my curiosity?"

"Sorry, trade secret," I said smugly. But inside I

realized my Kaolack idea wouldn't have worked if it hadn't been for Plan Z. This girl was a super-pro and I'd have to remember that. I should have known that by now, but her damn femaleness kept getting in the way.

"You have depths I still don't know about," she mused. "Back to the story, there was a little trouble at your office and at your place on Goree because somebody else had people there, too. There were some broken bodies left around, I'm afraid. Before dawn I had to admit defeat. I knew you were going to get across somehow. I called Circe and she released me from the contract. She told me to go ahead and follow this up to find out what's going on. And to cooperate with you in any way I saw fit." Flashing teeth. Hand on mine. Sincere and intimate voice. Sex radiation.

No, that's not a figure of speech. Darla has this thing she can do. She has this luscious body and a really sweet face, which should be enough to turn any man on. But she also has a way of ... of what? The best thing I can say is that she is able to project an almost palpable field of raw sexuality like a willing bitch in heat. And she can turn it on and off at will. I felt it like a crawling sensation on my skin and my loins began shouting "Go-Go-Go!" I've read that in the States they are studying energy fields around the body and even taking pictures of them, though they can't decide exactly what they are. And I remember my *okora* telling me something about them. But this woman had it under control. I'd seen Rocky use it on Demba, too. Right now, however, I was fortunate because I wasn't alone. Salif almost hit a boulder on the side of the road and the soldier broke out in a fit of coughing, so she had to turn it off. Then I got very scared. Very, very scared. For the first time I realized that she could actually influence my natural desire enough to completely blind my intellect. Up to now I had always convinced myself that even when I gave in to her it was because I wanted to. Now I knew that it was my body that wanted to, not me. "I" just went along with it. Which could be permanently fatal if she wasn't in a friendly mood. My God, this woman had power! There were some things in this world I was going to have to find more about. In the meantime, my best bet would be to avoid being alone with her.

Darla laughed as if she could read my thoughts. "I'm on your side now, honey. Something big is going on and we'll have to work together to find out what it is. Close together," she added, moving her thigh next to mine and giving me a little zap of power plus.

"Look, there's the fort," I said, idiotically. Of course it was the fort. That's where Salif had been heading. However, when a beautiful woman who frightens you goes on the make, rational thinking is often submerged. Doubt it? Then you have problems, friend. At any rate my diversion diverted her, momentarily.

We descended from the Land Rover and the guard took me to the *commandant,* the guy in charge, a friend from previous visits who was something like a governor of the province. Darla had gone out to the courtyard. Abdullah Benamar was waiting for me in his little official office with the desk and chairs left over from the colonial days. The greetings were formal and he carefully checked my passport and visa, asking me how long I intended to stay. As he went through the motions I looked at him with admiration. The Mauritanians are a very good looking people, the men exceptionally handsome and the women strikingly beautiful before they are fattened up for marriage or aged with hard work. They are mostly Berber with a mixture of Arab blood, and are the original Moors who overran Spain and established the magnificent culture that still influences that country. Today they retain a grace of manner and hospitality that is almost oriental.

Benamar finished his paperwork. "Now we can relax." He smiled with gleaming teeth. "It is good to see you again, *mon ami*. You come here too seldom. Let us have some tea." With this he got up and led me out of the official office to his private office. He was much more at ease here in his traditional setting. Four mattresses were positioned around a brown and white wool rug in the center of the room. As he sat down cross-legged, Benamar's white desert robe billowed in the breeze from a windowless window looking out over a deep, sandy valley. I sat on the next mattress and leaned on a highly-decorated leather pillow, a specialty of Mauritanian craftsmanship. My host clapped his hands and two servants came running in. One held a brazier and the makings for tea, and the other had two large glasses of a white foamy substance. "For refreshment while the tea is being prepared."

I laughed and took one of the glasses. "I look

forward to it. The day is warm and *zrit* is one of my favorite drinks." *Zrit,* if you've never been to Mauritania, is cool fresh milk, usually from a cow or camel. The servant stood looking at me with eyes glittering in anticipation. No doubt that is because *zrit* has another ingredient which is supposed to endow the drinker with outstanding virility. It is laced with camel urine. The Moors always seem to get a kick out of "Europeans" drinking it. I downed it and smacked my lips. "Delicious," I declared. The servant howled with laughter, took the glasses and skipped out of the room. It really isn't too bad once you get used to it and learn to stop your thinking processes while you drink it.

As the other servant prepared the tea Benamar and I had an informal talk. "It's a strange group you bring with you this time, Monsieur Loring. The old archeologist is not a surprise, but his 'assistant' doesn't seem to be what she claims. Forgive me, but if you were not a friend I would not even mention it. I have seen dozens of archeologists pass through here on their way to Aoudaghost and she is either the rankest of amateurs or she is playing a role. In my opinion, which you may counter, it is the latter." He stretched out comfortably and propped his arm on a pillow. "Interestingly, there seem to be two actresses on this safari. The red-headed one with the body of an *houri* is not as empty-headed as she pretends to be. She has the poor pilot smitten out of his senses and I have seen the look of a lioness in her eyes, when she wasn't aware I was watching. She gives me a curious impression. As you know I was once a guerrilla. This woman reminds me of our leader. I have the feeling she has already assessed the defense capabilities of this fort and decided on her escape plan, should such become necessary." He paused and sighed. "But then, I am getting old and perhaps I am a victim of fantasy. Perhaps they are both only pretty women who feel out of place in this strange land." He looked at me inquisitively.

"Perhaps," I answered noncommittally. Then I smiled slightly. "And perhaps not." I was glad to have Benamar's opinion. He was a brilliant politician and diplomat and capable of governing far more than the nowhereland of Tamchakett. The only trouble was that he wasn't quite as brilliant as the president of the country, who had shipped him out here to calm down his ambitions for awhile. With his suspicions already aroused it would be easy to have him either lock Darla up or ship her out, but my gut told me she could be helpful in unraveling the mystery of Benedetti. As for Maria, Benamar would gladly assign two guards to her "for her own protection," if I asked. But then how would I find out what she intended? So I just sat and smiled.

Benamar leaned forward and looked me in the eyes. "You are a friend," he said softly, "but this is my country and my province. If you know of anything that might bring trouble, I would consider it an act of friendship for you to tell me. If you know and do not tell me, I would consider it an act of..." He leaned back. "Foolishness," he completed.

I didn't want to compromise Benamar, but on the other hand I didn't want to compromise my chances of finding out what was up, either. So I told him part of the truth. "I have my suspicions, too. Unfortunately, at the moment that's all they are. I've been hired to take the two archeologists to Aoudaghost and the red-head is a friend of the pilot. When I know more I promise to let you know. Fair?"

"If I were you..." Sadly, I would never find out what he would do if he were me. Go home? Sell my business and retire to Tahiti? Write a play? It didn't matter. At that moment a servant announced the arrival of two visitors who came in right behind as if they were very familiar with the place. They were Chinese.

Benamar got up to escort them in and I stood politely. He made the introductions. "Monsieur Loring, may I present Dr. Chang and his assistant, Monsieur Chu. Dr. Chang is head of the medical team at Aioun. Monsieur Loring is a professional guide who knows the desert well." The two Chinese bowed slightly and I bowed even more slightly. I hadn't missed Benamar's subtlety. In the world of diplomacy, those of lesser rank are introduced to the person of higher rank. For his own reasons Benamar had made me out to be more than just a professional guide. It made the Chinese wary and gave Benamar a psychological edge.

By now the tea was ready, and two more glasses were brought forth. I said that the Mauritanians had something Oriental about them. Their method of preparing and serving tea enhanced that feeling. They had made it into an art.

During the tea ceremony I took a good look at the Chinese. They were from Communist China, of course. It didn't take the high-collared uniforms and red Mao buttons to tell me that, though. I knew that

Mauritania had opened diplomatic relations with Red China and that in return they had sent several teams of medical personnel under a technical assistance agreement. Dr. Chang wore a dark blue outfit and was a little rotund. His manner was open and friendly, even though he soon realized that I was an American. As he put the official line, "It is only with the American Government that we have a quarrel, not with the people." Chu, on the other hand, was coldly hostile. He said nothing—for all I knew he didn't even speak French—but he never took his penetrating eyes off me for one moment. His outfit was grey and I got the distinct impression that he was boss, a not uncommon arrangement among the Chinese. Conversation was bland until Benamar mentioned that I was taking the archeologists to Aoudaghost.

"Ah, yes, the old ruins that are somewhere north of here," said Chang. "I have wanted to see them since I arrived. I have been to the ones at Koumbi Saleh, you know, the capital of the ancient Ghana Empire, but I understand that although Aoudaghost is smaller the ruins are in a better state of preservation."

I nodded. "That's right. The last French team uncovered an entire mosque." I slurped up the last of my second glass of tea and tossed it back to the tea-maker. "So you have an interest in archeology, Doctor?"

"Yes. When I was younger I participated in some of the expeditions into our Gobi Desert. Of course, the civilizations there were much older, but just as decadent as many of the ones today." He looked significantly at Benamar. "At least the newest governments of the world are going to change all that, aren't they *commandant*?"

Benamar smiled. He was too wily to fall into an anti-American stand with Chang, and too smart also to do the opposite. The official Mauritanian position in world politics was to follow its own best interests. Survival is the name of that game. So he replied, "The newest governments will certainly change things, though what those changes will be, only Allah knows." Neat. Didn't offend anyone and established his independence at the same time. Even Chang laughed in appreciation.

It occurs to me that you might wonder why Benamar would have to be so careful about a political conversation way out in the middle of the desert. Dear innocents, when officials of two different governments have even a casual conversation (there is really no such thing in the world of diplomacy) they have to report it in detail to their superiors. If Benamar had seemed to side with the Chinese it would have been interpreted as a sign of growing support for Chinese policy in spite of official statements. If Benamar had seemed to side with me, then the Chinese would see that a friendly superior in the Mauritanian government found out and he would have been reprimanded. In fact, he might have been replaced, because the Chinese would undoubtedly have expressed their opinion that I was a CIA agent. In their eyes every American overseas is a CIA agent. So you see, diplomacy is far more than pushing cookies. But the paperwork is a pain.

Back to the party. We were finishing our third glass of tea when Chang did what I was half beginning to suspect he would. "*Commandant,* I am on my way to the capital, but there's no rush. Do you think it would be possible for us to accompany this little expedition to Aoudaghost for a night or two? I'd like very much to see it."

In the face of such a blunt request Benamar would have to have good official reason for refusing it, and he didn't. So he dropped it into my lap. "I have no opposition, but Monsieur Loring is in charge of the expedition. You'll have to ask him." He smiled as he waited to see what I would do. I didn't do anything. I just sat there worrying over the godawful coincidence of a Chinese amateur archeologist popping up minutes after my arrival. It was enough to give me goosebumps in spite of the heat. Especially since I don't believe in coincidences.

Finally, Chang asked, "Well, Monsieur Loring? I promise not to get in the way. It is just to indulge an old hobby. And who knows?" he smiled, "it might help to improve relations between our two countries."

Far be it from me to create an international incident, even though I was certain that Chang wouldn't even alter a facial expression without an order from higher up. So I passed the buck. "Actually, I'm just the organizer. The man in charge is Professor Aliberti. It's him we'll have to ask."

"The rest of your people are in the courtyard," put in Benamar. He stood and we all did the same. "Come along, Doctor Chang, Monsieur Chu, and I'll introduce them to you." The *commandant* let them pass in front and held me back till they were out of earshot. Quickly he whispered, "Chu is not what you think, not the leader."

"What is he?" I whispered back. Benamar solemnly drew his forefinger across his neck. Great, I thought. A hatchet man.

In the courtyard the soldiers had set up a large open-sided tent where the others were escaping from the assault of the sun. We ducked under the edge and sat on the thick, wool rug while intros were done. This time Benamar set Chang up as the bigger wheel. I watched Maria for any sign of reaction to the presence of the Chinese. Except for ordinary interest there didn't seem to be any. So I just watched Maria. Unlike Darla, her clothes were purely functional, all proper and expensively cut khaki with no unbuttoned front showing her bazooms. Aesthetically, I was a little sorry about that, but I had to admire the practicality of it. She was still a beautiful woman. So much so that it made you want to look around for the movie cameras. Even out here and dressed for digging she looked too good to be true. I gave my greetings to everyone and turned back to her.

"Well, when do you think you'd like to get started?"

"I think we're ready now." She turned to the professor. "Dr. Aliberti, are we ready to go to the site?"

"Yes! Of course we're ready. That's what we came here for. There is much work to do and we must get started right away in order to finish it." The cranky old bastard was as nice as ever.

Now Chang took the opening. "Dr. Aliberti, I am

an amateur archeologist and I'd like to join you at your site for a couple of days. Not just as a visitor. As a helper. I've done a fair amount of site work in the Gobi and I think I could be of assistance to you. I would consider it a privilege."

"But Professor, we have the work all arranged. A change in the scheduling might delay us." Maria's voice didn't show worry. Just concern.

"Nonsense, my dear. Experienced help is always welcome. Thank you, Dr. Chang. I'd be delighted to have you join us. And perhaps you could share some of your experiences in the Gobi with me." The two of them then launched into a discussion of archeological comparisons. I lent a partial ear to it and Chang sounded authentic, which caused me more worry because to my way of thinking that meant careful planning.

What worried me more now, though, was Maria. I was certain she was phony. Having met quite a few artifact hunters I notice that they are all budget-minded and that they adore volunteers who pay their own way and know what they're doing. Actually, I had hoped that Aliberti would turn Chang down to maintain professional secrecy about what he was going to do, but I miscalculated the effect that Chang's Gobi experience would have on him. But Maria neither wanted a volunteer nor was she worried about budgeting, as my fee showed. I wasn't happy. Believe me, mysteries do not excite me. They just make life complicated. I like things nice and neat and clear and open and simple. Is that asking too much?

"... too much!" Maria's low voice startled me.

"This expedition is turning into a party. It was only supposed to be you and I and the professor. Now there are the Chinese and that shameless redhead and probably the pilot, too." She took one of my hands in both of hers. "Lee, can't you do something? It's going to be hard for us to find time alone together with all these people about. Use some authority."

"Sorry, love. I don't own the desert. My job is to get you and the professor to the site, watch over you, and get you back to Dakar. I can't do anything about the Chinese. Maybe I can get the pilot and his girl to stay here, though." I detached myself and moved over to where Darla was cuddled up with Jean-Pierre, the pilot. The poor guy was drunk on her vibes. "Jean-Pierre, I want you to stay here with the plane. Unless you want to fly this young lady back and return. We're going to be here for a week, you know."

"Oh sure, *mon ami*," he said, and no one saw Darla stick her tongue out at me. It was a cheap trick and it wouldn't work, but I wanted to see what she would do. J-P looked at her and his eyes glazed over. "Do you want me to fly you back, *cherie*?"

"My goodness, I don't think so. My tour doesn't leave for another three weeks and I've never been anyplace like this before, all wild and stuff. It's sure different than Charleston." Try to imagine the equivalent of a cute Southern accent in French and you've got it. She was playing the innocent tourist bit, an almost infallible turn-on.

"Good," said J-P. "Then she will stay here with me." He squeezed her leg.

"Oh, but Jean-Pierre, can't I even go out to see what a ruin looks like? I can just go out and take a look and come right back."

"How are you going to do that?" I asked. "It's forty kilometers out and I'm afraid I can't spare the gas for two extra trips."

"Why, I can go with the soldiers. I heard that nice commander or whatever tell the soldiers to go out and help you set up the tents and then come back. Jean-Pierre, is it all right if I do that? I'll just ride out and back and that's all. Okay?" How much sugar could he take?

"Well, I don't know if I want you to ride out with those soldiers dressed the way you are."

"No problem at all! I brought a change of clothes." She jumped up. "I'll go put on something more modest and be right back. Thanks, Jean-Pierre." She gave him a peck on the lips and away she went.

J-P looked slightly confused. "How did that happen?"

"Don't let it bother you. Adam had the same problem." I patted him on the back and stood. *"Monsieur le commandant,"* I called to where Benamar was still talking with Chang and Aliberti, "with your permission I would like to get this safari on the road so that we can set up camp before dark."

"Of course, Monsieur Loring." He clapped his hands and two soldiers came running. He gave them orders in Hassania, the Arab-Berber dialect used in Mauritania, and they ran off to help ready the vehicles. In a bustle of movement we all went outside.

"Miss Benedetti and Dr. Aliberti, you'll ride with me. I assume your stuff is already loaded? Fine. Dr. Chang, do you and your companion have everything you need for an overnight stay?"

"For several nights, if necessary, Monsieur Loring. We were on our way to the capital, remember."

Sure you were. "Okay, you can follow us. *Commandant,* are the soldiers coming, too?"

"Yes, but only to help you set up your camp. Then they are to return. And I told the lovely young friend of your pilot that she could go along for the ride. You don't object?"

"No, I don't mind," I lied. And then I figured that if she really didn't want to kill me any more, maybe she could be some help.

Darla came out of the fort at that moment. "All right, I'm ready." And she was. She no longer looked like a pin-up from *Argosy*. Now she wore a khaki jump suit with lightweight suede boots, a practical cotton scarf and a webbed belt with a small canvas pouch. That pouch could contain anything from a tiny pistol or mini-grenades to emergency rations for an extended desert stay. Or possibly, just possibly, band-aids and sunburn ointment.

Sounding like her hackles were raised, Maria said, "You seem to have come well prepared for a spontaneous trip."

"Oh, mother always taught me to be prepared for anything," replied Darla brightly. "I was saving this outfit for my Cairo trip, but I'm so interested in old ruins. Like you." Angelic smile.

Maria coolly ignored the double-entendre. "My

interest is professional. And an archeological site is not a playground. Children can get hurt, so please be careful." Without giving Darla a chance for rebuttal, she got into my Rover with Aliberti. Women can be cute.

Everyone was finally ready to go. Just before I got into my car I stopped to have a word with Darla in the last vehicle. In English I said, "Watch Chu. He kills."

She nodded her head. "With his hands. And you watch Maria."

"Why?" I grinned, thinking I had stirred some jealousy.

With a solemn face, "She kills, too."

I spent the whole time on the road to Aoudaghost sincerely wishing I had stayed home.

Aliberti spent it chattering happily about what he was going to do once we got there. He and Maria talked about where they would set up the surveying equipment and what measurements they would take and how he would be a smash hit at the convention. As far as I could tell his big thesis had to do with the original population of Aoudaghost. Aliberti thought it was Bafour, a mysterious people now disappeared from West Africa, while most of his colleagues thought it was blacks from the Ghana Empire. All I knew was that there was a cave near the site with crude paintings of men in chariots chasing giraffes. Since there are no longer any giraffes in West Africa, that told me the place had to be *very* old. I wondered if any archeologists had even looked at the cave

The only thing that interrupted the merry

conversation in the back seat was the bumps. Everytime we hit our heads on the roof there would be a brief lull in the talk. Roads in Mauritania are something else. Whatever they are, they aren't roads. Mostly they are tracks in the sand that change with every gust of wind. At best they are the space between two lines of stones set on rocky outcroppings, with only the stones to designate the difference between the "road" and the surrounding terrain. At worst, they were living, twisting things that reached up and grabbed hold of your car and shook it and you to pieces. Mauritania is the only place I know of where the roads themselves are accidents. A particularly vicious bump nearly took off our rear axle. That was the sign. We had arrived in Aoudaghost.

6/Aoudaghost

Aoudaghost. What a name to conjure up mystery, intrigue, adventure. But there ain't much there, folks. It's a small, sort of open-ended valley by some rocky outcroppings that are too low to be called mountains and too sharp-edged to be called hills. Desert scrub, sand and hillocks, plus an ancient well by the remnants of a waterway. That was Aoudaghost now. Oh, and the reason we were all there. The ruins. Be careful you don't dream up visions of great crumbling temples a la Egypt or Ankor Wat. The ruins at Aoudaghost are not impressive at all. In fact, there is practically nothing above ground. There are the remains of the mosque that I mentioned before and a couple other diggings, a fair amount of potsherds, and an untouched graveyard (excavation is forbidden by the government). Not exactly an archeologist's paradise, but it turned some of them on. Like Aliberti, who had rushed off to take his measurements as soon as I had brought the Rover to a halt.

Chang went with Aliberti while the rest of us set up camp in a flat circular area used by all the visitors. As we worked with the tents and the gear I felt something nagging at my brain. The place didn't seem quite right. It didn't look any different than it had on my last visit over a year ago, but there was something missing. Salif and I finished our tent and helped Maria with hers and the professor's. The soldiers unloaded the supplies and set up the *guerbas*, water-filled goatskins hung on wood frames that would provide us with water cooled by evaporation. I had an extra one set up by my tent for cooling my beer. Meanwhile, Darla stood around in wide-eyed wonder as if she had never even been in Girl Scouts. I was certain she could have set up the camp blindfolded in half the time it took us.

Still nagged by the feeling that something was amiss, I questioned one of the soldiers. "Moustapha, does this place seem right to you?"

"No, *patron*." He called me 'boss' because I was in charge of the party.

"What's wrong with it?"

"No sheep, no goats, no tents."

That was it! In this season there should have been nomads using the well. It was highly unusual not to have them around. "Is the water bad?" I sure hoped not. If it were we'd either have to cut the trip short or use precious gasoline getting water from Tamchakett.

Moustapha shouted an order to his companion, who ran off to check the well. We waited until he came back. When he did it was with a smile on his face. In Hassania he told Moustapha that the water was okay.

"Then where are the nomads?" I asked.

"Don't know, *patron*. Maybe at another well. Will have to report to the *commandant*."

It was odd, but I shrugged it off. I supposed it was possible that we had just caught the nomads between trips. I walked back with the soldiers to their Rover. They were ready to go. Darla had a camera and was taking a picture of Salif in front of a tent, just like a tourist. "Darla," I shouted, "it's time to go." Would she or wouldn't she?

"Oh, I've decided to stay. Here's a note these nice soldiers can give to Jean-Pierre."

Have you ever felt relief and uneasiness at the same time? It's a curious sensation. No one but Darla has ever stimulated it in me. "Uh, but you don't have a tent."

"Well, now," she said as she came up and put her hands on my shoulders, "that can be easily fixed. You sleep in the Land Rover and I'll sleep with Salif." Impish smile.

"Go to hell, woman," I answered, taking her arms down.

"Well, then, you can take Salif with you and I'll sleep in the tent alone." Eyes wide, innocent expression.

"That won't do either," I began.

"Darling!" she said in her lowest, sexiest mock-shocked voice," are you suggesting that you and I . . . I mean we two . . . the two of us together . . ." She made a 'for shame' sign with her fingers the way kids do.

Maria was watching us with her usual amusement. I think I got a little red in the face, not an easy trick when you have a dark tan. "You will either sleep in the Land Rover," I said with what I felt at the time was controlled fury, but which Darla much later told me sounded like a quavering old man, "or you will return right now with the soldiers!"

Darla backed away, her eyes downcast. "Yessir," she gave in meekly. "You're the *patron* and I'm only here on your sufferance. I'll sleep in the cold and lonely Land Rover if you want me to. Or I'll sleep on the ground where the scorpions can bite me. Or in the well. If you say so I'll climb a tree..."

I turned away from her in total exasperation and told the soldiers they could go. Benamar said he would send them back in a week to see how we were getting along. After they left I started to check the camp to see if everything was in order. The wind sometimes blew hard at night and tent pegs had better be secure. Maria fell in beside me. Chu was sitting stoney-faced in front of his and Chang's tent so I didn't bother with it. I think I would have enjoyed it if their tent had blown away.

Once out of Chu's earshot, Maria asked me, "What are the Chinese doing here?"

I raised an eyebrow. "Chang's an amateur archeologist and he just..."

Maria interrupted me with an unladylike expletive. "That is too pat, that he should turn up right now." She seemed to hesitate, as if deciding what to say next. "I think he's here to sabotage Dr. Aliberti's work."

I didn't think that she thought that. I thought that she thought that... wait a minute until I untwist my tongue. I felt that Maria was worried about something other than Aliberti's work, but I played along. "Are you going to warn the professor?"

"Yes, as soon as he gets back. Meantime," she put a hand on my arm, "I want to make up for being so cool toward you. You are a very exciting man and I am not as aloof as I have pretended to be." Wet lips.

The temperature outside was over a hundred. Inside I began to match it. There is something about a direct approach by a beautiful woman that stirs my blood. Warning bells in my head went ping, ping, ping, but my body told them to shut up. I couldn't imagine any danger this early in the trip. Which just shows you that the best of us fantasizers can suffer a lack of imagination from time to time. Unfortunately, this time was very nearly fatal for me. But of course it wasn't quite fatal or I wouldn't be here to tell you about it. Someone else would have told you, probably in an entirely different way, with a different title, and not nearly as interestingly... okay, okay, I'll go on.

I considered. "We could go into my tent, but that would be rather blatant. And a blanket in the bushes would be very uncomfortable at this time of day."

Almost offhandedly, she said, "I heard there was a cave nearby."

Right, the cave! It would be perfect. "Yes, there is a cave. Not many people know about it. C'mon," I took her hand, "let me show it to you." Pant, pant.

I led her into the path that led to the cave. It followed a route behind some tall bushes, so no one could actually see where we were going. The cave was at the top of a steep, but walkable, cliff. From below it only looked like a discoloration in the rock, and you had to get quite close before realizing what it was. Unless someone showed it to you or you discovered it by accident, you would never know it was there.

It took us a half hour of climbing to reach it. The entrance was no more than a horizontal slit about five feet high at the widest. Inside was a flat rock that took up most of the space. Behind the rock were several feet of bat guano, but there were no bats here now. On the ceiling and walls were paintings in reds, yellows, blacks and browns. Coyotes, lions, deer, rabbits, hippos, giraffes, and those men in what looked to me like chariots. For untold centuries the area had been uninhabitable for most of the animals portrayed, and chariots were never supposed to have been here.

We ducked into the cave and I stopped. I liked it here and had spent hours studying the paintings and imagining what the desert must have been like when they were made. But something was different now. I felt a prickling over the whole front of my body, as if I had walked into a field of static electricity. It didn't look any different. However, the feeling was strong. Then my whole body shivered.

"What's wrong?" Maria put an arm around me, nuzzled my neck. "Are you getting nervous?"

I suppose I should have been nervous with Maria changing from ice to fire, but as I said, I thought it was too early for danger. And besides, my God, what a bod'! How could I turn that down? No, it wasn't Maria who was causing the prickles. "Don't you feel anything?"

"I feel you, Lee. What else am I supposed to feel?" She turned me toward her, wrapped her arms around me, ground her hips against mine and kissed me right out there in broad daylight. In the shadow of the cave, really. What the hell. It made me forget about the prickles.

We made long, lazy love on the flat rock, using our clothing as padding. Maria was a demanding lover, with a tendency toward scratching during her heights. I scratched back. Not enough to mar her olive bronze skin, though. What a fiery pleasure she was. She was almost as good a lover as me. We played Antelope Rag, Australian Roll, and a minor variation on the Tahitian Special. She put herself wholeheartedly into sex, and was more than competent, but I found myself exploding with feeling that was generated by something beyond her skill.

Finally, we rested in a seated position with her facing me and her legs over mine. Gradually, the prickling sensation made itself felt all over my back. "There's something in this cave," I stated.

"There sure is," she said, disentangling her legs and reaching for some object in her trouser pocket. "It brings out the beast in you." The object was a mirror. I chuckled inwardly at the vanity of women even on a safari. She fluffed her hair and smoothed out her cheeks as she held the little mirror before her. By now the sun was low enough to shine directly into the cave. I saw flashes of light in the brush miles away and idly noted that she must have a two-sided mirror. "You're one of the best lovers I've ever had. I'm sorry this trip will be so short."

"So am I, love." I kissed her shoulder. Two weeks

with Maria would just be getting started, I thought. Then I felt the prickling again. I turned toward the back of the cave. My face prickled. "There's something in here that's giving me a funny feeling." I bent over the edge of the flat rock toward the heap of guano. Half buried in it was a gray canvas bag. "Hey, there's a sack." I reached down to pick it up. "Maybe this is what..."

Whappo! Something hard and heavy connected with the back of my neck. I felt no pain. Just darkness covering my eyes and a slow, floating sensation as I headed for the guano. "Oh, shit!" was my last coherent thought.

From what I was told much later, this is a reconstruction of what happened while I was in the land of Nod:

Maria checked to make sure that I was really out. I was. She had a mean way with a rock. Then she picked up the bag and quickly got dressed. To slow me down in case I woke up she also gathered up my clothes and took them with her as she made her way down the slope. When she arrived at the camp, everything was quiet. No one was in sight. It made her wonder, but she supposed everyone was at the worksite. Confidently, she went to her tent, threw back the flap, ducked inside and froze.

"Greetings, Miss Benedetti," said Chang in English. He was sitting cross-legged with a gun pointed at her belly. Seeing a quick tensing of her muscles, he remarked, "Do not attempt anything childish. Chu is at your back." This was emphasized by the feel of a knife point next to her spine.

"I didn't expect you to move so soon." Her voice

was calm and relaxed. She held the bag in front of her. "Is this what you want?"

Chang moved the muzzle of the gun sharply upward in the direction of her head, and smiled. "That is one of the things I want, yes. Set it down very slowly and carefully. Slowly!" She did as she was told and straightened up. "You will now back slowly out of the tent. Make the slightest movement to defend yourself and you will die in great pain."

Maria backed out and stood in the late sunlight with Chu's knife still touching her back. She went over a dozen escape tactics in her mind and realized they were all useless in the present circumstance. "What else do you want?" she asked. "That sack contains the key to everything."

"You will soon see. Walk over to my tent."

As they walked, Maria planned to make her counterattack as soon as she got inside the tent. Chu would be in a vulnerable position as he ducked in after her, and maybe she could turn things to her advantage. But this hopeful thought was squelched when Chang entered first to await her entrance. He was a professional who wasn't taking any chances. She bent down, went in, and gave an involuntary gasp of surprise. Darla was spread-eagled on her stomach on the floor of the tent, still fully clothed. Her wrists and ankles were tied to stakes driven through the canvas floor of the tent. A gag was tied tightly over her mouth, forcing her lips apart, and a pillow had been shoved uner her hips to raise them off the ground. Maria noted the bruises on her face and several tears in her clothes where angry welts showed through. Looking at Chu, now, she saw a bloody gash along his jaw. The girl had tried hard, she thought. Had she known the truth she might have been a little more in awe of Chu. Any man who could take Darla in a fight had to be extremely good.

At last Maria saw the other four stakes already set up. She whipped around to face Chang, feeling the warning bite of Chu's knife and seeing the alert reaction of Chang's gun hand. "Surely you're not planning to rape me!" What they did to Darla was of no concern.

"Surely, we are," smiled Chang. "We have spent long months without women, apart from a few unbathed Moorish children. Sex is a basic necessity, and it will be a great pleasure to enjoy two adult women."

"Do what you want with the other girl," Maria made her voice sultry. "You'll find that with me, rape is unnecessary. I'm obviously under your control. I'll do anything you like." She must stay free, if possible.

"I happen to like rape," said Chang simply. "You will now lie down on your back and allow Chu to tie you to the stakes."

It wasn't a matter of choice. Maria lay down and Chu bound her expertly in place. She had no fear. It was an ordeal she had gone through before and could take again. It would be over soon, she knew. Sooner than Chang thought. But she might be able to delay it with words. "I thought the Party frowned on indiscriminate sex."

"The Party thinking on that matter refers to Chinese women. Foreign devils," he used the Chinese term for whites, "do not count. Raise your hips so that Chu may place a pillow under them. Do not hesitate. You can be raped while bleeding, if necessary. I enjoy rape, but I do not believe in making it more difficult than it has to be."

Now Maria felt completely helpless. She began to worry. Were Chang and his cohort the type who liked torture, too? The timing was so close. They would be here in a little while. "And what happens after the rape? Murder?"

"Oh, of course not. I have no intention of harming either of you. I will leave you tied here when we leave. Mr. Loring's driver is tied up in another tent." Chu slipped his knife inside her blouse, slicing away the buttons and cutting her bra in half. "I assume you killed Loring?" Chu pulled her blouse apart, exposing her breasts.

Maria closed her eyes and tried to remain calm. This was not simply rape, it was calculated humiliation. Torture of a different kind. "Yes, I killed him. He was of no further use." She knew it wasn't true. But if Loring stumbled into camp it would divert their attention and give her more time. Time was what she wanted!

Chang looked thoughtful. "Then I wonder why you brought his clothes back. To slow down a dead man?" Chu put his knife to her belt, cut through it. Then he ripped her trousers open along each side down to her knees. "Don't bother to answer. I'm sure he's not dead. Yet. In a little while, Mr. Chu will go and give him an accident. Meanwhile, let us see what the sex of a Soviet agent looks like." Chang reached out and slowly drew the center portion of her trousers and pants down until it fell loosely between her legs. Her mound was high, her hair was lush and black. "Quite a forest," said Chang.

You yellow pig! she hissed to herself. Calmly, she said aloud, "I have nothing to do with the Soviets." The denial was futile, but it bought precious time.

"Nonsense. Your cover has been excellent, but not good enough for our Secret Service. You did have Aliberti completely convinced." Chang touched a finger to her navel and traced the hairline that stretched upward from between her legs. "A shame about the professor. Had a stroke just as I was becoming convinced of his innocence." Chang's finger reached her pubic hair, ventured further, entered and rested inside her. "He was innocent, wasn't he?"

Maria's face burned with anger and shame. To be forced to talk like this... "Aliberti was only a tool."

"I believe you this time. Not that it matters." Chang gestured to Chu, who moved astride Darla. "Watch this," Chang said to Maria. "I want to see and feel your reactions."

Methodically, Chu cut away Darla's shirt, and then began on her trousers. "Is this what you call pleasure?" asked Maria with disdain. Chu appeared to be cutting away the skin of an animal.

"You will keep your mouth shut unless I tell you to open it. You will have a chance to open it shortly." In a moment Darla's clothes were lying in rags around her, naked buttocks pushed high in the air by the pillow. Chu started to strip. Maria fought hard for detachment, but her body betrayed her. Chang noticed the flush on her skin, her rising nipples, the first beginnings of moisture. He chattered away as if they were merely having afternoon tea.

"When we leave, we will pay a visit to the *commandant* and tell him you are coming along nicely. Of course, you will not be able to follow right away. The air has been let out of your tires and all your gasoline has mysteriously leaked away. I suppose you could try to walk to Tamchakett, but it would be much easier on you to wait for the soldiers to come at the end of the week." Chu was now kneeling between Darla's outstretched legs. "Either way, it won't matter. Chu and I have diplomatic immunity. No one would believe such an atrocious story as you could tell." Chang chuckled and moved his finger around. "No one would dare believe it."

Chu was rigidly ready. He parted Darla's buttocks and entered her the hard way. She gave a grunt of surprise and used her training to relax, to make it easier. For a while there were only the sounds to be expected from such a situation. After what seemed like an abnormally long time, Chu finished with Darla, but was not finished himself. He turned and looked hungrily at Maria. Chang moved aside and gestured for him to go ahead. If she had been able, she would have shrank back in revulsion. There was no shrinking back, however. She was open, exposed, available. Chu mounted her without hesitation. Maria spit at him, but he paid not the slightest attention. Methodical in this as in everything else, he worked until he spent himself with a sharp groan. Then he backed off and put on his clothes.

"The American, see that he is dead," Chang said to him. "He is the only one who could give us trouble." Chu left the tent and Chang turned back to

Maria. He took her breasts in both hands and squeezed them with a sigh. Then he sat up and began unbuttoning his shirt. "Chu is competent, but unimaginative. I have much more of a gourmet appetite, and I do not mind taking what the Americans call 'seconds.' First, I am going to..."

About this time I was coming out of my undesired snooze. My first awareness was of bat dung in my mouth. I spit it out and pulled my head up sharply. Next time I spit it out again and raised my head more gently. With tender care I opened my eyes and thought I had gone blind. Then an awareness of cool air made me realize the sun had set. I sat up and waited for the dizziness to pass. It wouldn't, so I cursed it. If I had three wishes, all three would be for a new head. Dizzy or not I knew I was going to have to stand up or sit in shit for the rest of my life. I struggled, I cussed, I groaned, I scrambled, I scratched, I did it! I stood.

What had happened? There was Maria, warm and luscious. There was a bag. And there was... ooooohhh, my head reminded me of what there was. Warm and luscious Maria had clobbered me. Had I done that badly? No, the bag must have had something to do with it. The bag that made me tingle. Maria had made me tingle, too. Not in quite the same way, but... Whoa! Stop. Straighten out the thoughts. Like a road. Like a road that goes on for miles and miles till it comes to a village and there is a... Maria clobbered me and took the bag. What else did she take? My virginity. No, you fool, it was a twelve-year-old girl down the block... God, stop it, please! Stop the pain!

Hours or minutes later, one of the two, I felt slightly better. Enough to notice that I was chilly. And Naked. I hunted for my clothes. Gently. My head was still punishing me for making it work. But there were no clothes around. Why had she taken my clothes? And why had she hit me? I'd have given her the goddamn bag if she'd asked! I clambered over the rock and slid down to the cave entrance. No sounds from down below. No glow of a campfire. I set my foot on the path and yelped. The noise ricocheted off the inside of my skull and echoed through my sinuses. I steadied myself and picked the sand burr out of my foot. They weren't supposed to be this far north, the little bastards. Sand burrs are one of the nastier inventions of Mother Nature. About a quarter-inch across with barbed spikes, they aren't good for anything but spreading pain and sand burrs. At least I knew why Maria took my boots. I didn't want to go down that path, but then I hadn't learned to fly, yet.

(Owowowowowowow) that was me whispering my pain as I hopped down the slope. I wasn't whispering so no one could hear me. At that moment I couldn't have cared less. I just didn't want my head to get mad at me. Near the bottom I was still hopping not so merrily along when something pulled on my left arm, flipped me up in the air and tossed me into a thorn bush. *Everything* complained now; my head, my nekkid body, and my broken arm. To top it off, I felt I was going to be killed in the next few seconds. Oh boy, I was in terrific shape.

I couldn't see my assailant, but I turned my head in the direction of a shuffle in the sand. A flashlight flicked on and a ghastly face appeared. It was Chu holding the light under his chin. What was really ghastly was that he was smiling. And his voice was enough to strike terror into a terrorist. "Mr. Loring, it is time for you to die. I am going to kill you." I have come to the conclusion that the intellect is of very little use in survival situations. There I was, bruised, battered and broken, about to be snuffed out, and all my intellect could do was say to me, 'Hey, how about that, he speaks English!'

And then his head exploded. Literally, it blew apart. For the tiniest instant I thought it was a trick before the sound of a rifle slammed past and bounced off the cliff. My intellect immediately said, 'Aha! Rescue!' But my body said, 'Hide!' I listened to my body. I scrambled off the path as far and fast as I could go, given my condition, and ended up in a rocky, uncomfortable spot overlooking the camp just before a wild bunch of camel riders came galloping up between the tents. In the starlight I could see Chang come running out of his tent, pulling up his pants. And I could see one of the riders reach down with the butt end of a rifle and knock him a good six feet without touching the ground. Then several of the riders got down and went looking in the tents. I was totally confused. Why was Chang the only one to come running out? Where were all the others? And who were the cameleers? In this light they appeared to be wearing black robes and turbans, but I knew these would be the indigo-dyed garments of the so-called Blue People of the deep desert. Which tribe, though? Who would raid a camp this close to government protection?

I sat there, not only in confusion but in great pain, watching a bound Salif being pulled out of one tent and various supplies out of others. A raider went into Chang's tent and rushed back outside to call excitedly to the one man still on a camel. The latter leaped right off the standing camel and dashed into the tent. I wasn't very far away, so voices were quite clear. The language was Italian.

"My God!" The voice of the man who had run into the tent sounded vaguely familiar.

"Put your jaw and your eyes back in place and untie me!" I heard Maria say in a commanding tone.

"What happened? Who is this other woman?"

"Never mind that for now! There was a Chinese who ran out of this tent when you arrived. Where is he?"

"Outside on the ground. Unconscious. Should I untie this woman?"

"Leave her where she is. She may be a tourist or she may be something else. Get me some clothes. And keep your bandits from sacking my tent. I want to use it."

"I brought the desert clothes you requested."

"Get them!"

I saw the Italian come out and give some orders to two men who were just leaving Maria's tent with their arms full. They turned around and threw the stuff back in. He went to the saddle bag on his camel and brought something back to Maria, probably her clothes. I wished I knew what had been going on. What were Maria and apparently Darla doing tied up in Chang's tent? And Maria had seemed to expect the arrival of this troop. The plot was getting as thick as taffy. I shivered. It was getting cold and I was nude. My arm was throbbing with pain and a dull ache enveloped my head and shoulders. Intellect said to surrender and at least I'd get some clothing and my arm taken care of. They might even turn out to be friendly. Body said to suffer, it's safer. Good ol' body. Even in bad shape it could think straight.

From Maria, "There was another Chinese..."

"One of the men shot him in the head. He was holding a flashlight."

"He was heading up a path to a cave where I left Loring unconscious. You'd better send some men up to see if he's still there."

The Italian's head popped out of the tent and he gave some orders in a dialect I didn't understand. Then he ducked back in and I heard him say, "You know, it's indecent to leave her uncovered like that."

"Then do the indecent thing, Romano, I really don't care." A dark shape that must have been Maria hurried out of Chang's tent and into her own.

Romano! My head reeled. He was supposed to be dead. Or it was supposed to be thought he was dead. At any rate, it was a very much alive Romano who was saying, "In a way I am sorry to take advantage of you in such a situation, my little dove, but opportunities like this do not come frequently." Then he became silent and I shivered some more.

The rest of the men, about five as far as I could tell, had pushed the Land Rovers on their sides and were piling tents and whatever gear they didn't want or couldn't carry around them. In a little while Romano came out of Chang's tent and shouted something else. The tribesmen gave a whoop and ran to where Darla was still bound. I found myself pitying her for the first time, and angry frustration at my helpless position dulled my pain.

Shortly, the two men who had been sent to the cave returned and talked to Romano. Three others had already come out of the tent where Darla was and these were immediately sent to get their rifles and were set up in guard positions around the outer edge of the camp. It was nice to see that Romano still thought highly of me. I thanked my guardian angel that he didn't know my whereabouts and status. I would be fair game for a blind midget with two hands and a foot tied behind her. The two from the cave went to have their turn with Darla. It was sure a tough night for her.

Maria came out of her tent dressed like the tribesmen, only with a white turban. Vanity. "Did they find Loring?"

"No, no sign of him. He's loose out there somewhere. I've set up guards."

"I'm not sure that will be necessary. He's naked and weaponless. Unless he was in the camp when you came."

"No one came out of the tents but the Chinese. If Loring had been in camp he would have at least freed the black. But he is dangerous with or without clothes. And anything can be used as a weapon."

Sure, I thought, I could always attack nine armed people with a rock, or I could use my broken arm as a club. Sometimes I get the feeling that my reputation is bigger than I am.

"The main thing is to keep him as helpless as possible. Send some men out to bring Aliberti's body back here. It's in an excavation about a hundred yards in that direction." Maria paused for a moment. "And bring me Chang."

"The Chinese? Right. I already tied him up. What happened to the professor? This whole operation seems to have gotten out of hand."

From where I was I could imagine how controlled fury was distorting Maria's lovely features. "No one requested your judgement of the operation. You have been paid to do a job. Do it and keep your mouth shut about anything else!"

Romano was not the type to take that from an ordinary woman, not even a beautiful one, but I saw him hesitate and then do what she commanded. Not long after Aliberti's body, wearing clothes I could have used, was brought into camp and dumped through the open door of Chang's overturned Land Rover. Romano had given other orders and the rest of the tents and gear were piled by the vehicles, too. Even the one Darla was in had been torn down and she had been bound hand and foot. I had seen her naked body as they took the tent down. I can't say I was shocked because I expected it, but more and more anger welled up in me. Salif had been tossed next to her.

Chang, now conscious, was being held by two men in front of Maria. "Well, Mr. Chang," she said in English, "your plan didn't quite work out." Her voice was calm and easy.

Taking heart from that, Chang replied, "Fortunes of war, Miss Benedetti. I assume you'll tie me up now and leave me with the others?"

"That's a false assumption, Mr. Chang. Within

the limited time that I have I'm going to make sure that you die a horrible death." She gestured to the men holding him and they threw him to the ground. To Romano she said in Italian, "I want his legs spread apart. Use more men if you have to."

Chang yelled and struggled. "You can't do this to me! I have diplomatic immunity! This is not done!"

Maria laughed. She laughed as she pulled out a dagger and knelt between Chang's legs. She laughed as she opened his trousers and cut off his genitals, and carelessly threw them into the bushes. Still chuckling as she wiped off the blood and gave Romano her next order. "Have them break his arms and legs and drop him into the Land Rover with Aliberti. Then make sure everything left in the camp is put on the pile, and I mean everything. I don't even want a sock left that Loring could use. Douse it all with gasoline from the Chinese jerricans and set fire to it."

Romano looked at Darla and Salif. "What about them?"

Without even turning from Chang, Maria said, "Have someone slit their throats and put them on the pile with the rest of the stuff."

It seemed to me that Romano either shrugged or shuddered before he gave the orders. I decided in that moment that I was going to have to die. What I intended to do was silly and useless, but I would do it. Before they slit any throats I was going to yell and give myself away. It would only stall the inevitable. There was no way for Darla or Salif to escape, but I couldn't sit here and watch them die. I didn't question whether I was doing it for them or for me. It was just what I was going to do.

Without emotion I watched as Chang's limbs were broken, and heard his pitiful cries as he was dropped into the Rover. Watched the men scour the camp for odds and ends to throw on the pile, and saw them pour the gasoline over it. It was time for them to turn their attention to the two figures on the ground. I picked up a rock in my good hand, intending to throw it to give emphasis to my yell. My throat muscles tensed.

And all the men gathered in a group and sounded like they were having an argument. Romano went over to them and they argued with him.

Impatiently, Maria said, "What is it? Have them take care of those two and let's get going!"

Romano came back to her. "It won't be as easy as that. They want to take the girl along for pleasure till they tire of her and they want to keep the black to sell as a slave."

An insertion for you, dear and gentle reader. Don't be skeptical. In the latter half of twentieth century Africa, slavery still exists. It's on a small scale and well hidden, but it's there.

"Impossible!" Maria blew up. "We must move out of here fast. We cannot afford to bring extra burdens. Tell them they are being well paid and I will not have our lives and the operation endangered just for their pleasure and profit!"

Romano went back to the group of men. More arguments and gesticulations. Once more Romano faced Maria. "I'm suggesting you do as they say. These Touaregs are independent as hell. They just might slit our throats if they're unhappy." Maria started to protest, but Romano stopped her. "Listen, there's more. You must be more practical. We'll be in the desert at least three weeks. You're a woman, and they don't care that much for the money you've promised them. They're in this more for the adventure anyway. I don't care what you do with your body, but I have no desire to die defending you if you decide you're not in the mood for a gang rape."

Maria strode over to the group of men. They backed away, as if in fear. One of them shouted to Romano.

"For some reason they're afraid of you, but that won't stop them from doing you in if they don't get their way," said the Italian. "I have to admit you're making me uneasy, too. You're different than when we last met. You're even different than when I found you earlier." Romano was silent a moment and then spoke up. "No matter. I say give them their way and let's go. Loring may be on his way to Tamchakett right now."

"It will take him two days to get there in his condition." More like a week, in my estimation. She paced back and forth a couple times. "All right. Let them take the girl and the black. Set fire to the pile and let's move. We'll go north until daybreak, and then east. In two days the wind will cover our tracks. Move!"

The pile was set afire and Darla and Salif were loaded onto camels like baggage. No reason for me to die right away, so I released my grip on the rock. At least they had a fighting chance for life a little longer.

Even while mounted, I could see the Touaregs

giving Maria a wide berth. That wasn't like them. They were wild and tough nomads, unafraid of anything except evil spirits, the desert djinn. I wasn't even too surprised to see them this far out of their normal territory. What power did she hold over them? The direction they took to leave brought them to within a few yards of my sanctuary. As Maria passed I felt the unmistakable tingling I had felt in the cave.

I waited until I was sure they had gone. Then I went down to the fire to warm up, and managed to save a scrap of tenting. Chang screamed for an awfully long time.

7/Desert

Morning. The pile of tents, gear and vehicles was just a charred heap of trash now. It was still warm, though, and I stayed close to it until the sun took the chill out of the air. Somewhere in the middle of that heap were the bones of Chang and Aliberti. Chang was no great loss to the world, but Aliberti had seemed like a good old man in spite of his crankiness. An old thought from childhood rose to the surface of my mind: 'It isn't fair that the innocent should get hurt.' A bit of anger that poor old Aliberti should have suffered from the wrongs of others came with it. Then more recent words, the words of my okora, rose up and swept the older ones away. "There are no victims," he had said to me once. "The *lindon* (soul) chooses its own death, even though the body rebels."

Of course, that went against everything I had ever been taught, but I latched on to it now because it was better than being angry about something I couldn't help.

I stood, stretched, and put the whole thing out of my mind. Heavy thoughts were okay in the security of a comfortable chair with a glass of cognac and a filled pipe, but at the moment I had to think about survival. I looked around to see what I could salvage, and was quickly disappointed. The Touaregs had been thorough even in the darkness. Apart from the scrap of tent I had saved, all I found was someone's wool sock. Debate time. Should I make a sling for my arm, which was swollen and subject to shooting pains whenever I moved, or should I make a cap for my head, which the sun would soon be hammering at? I finally opted for a cap. I needed a clear brain more than a comfortable arm. I took a long time to cut the sock in the right way with just one hand and the metal frame of a Rover. When it was finished my head was covered, but I was glad I wouldn't be seen by my friends.

Next decision. What to do with the scrap of tent? Sandals? That would give me some protection from sand burrs and hot sand. Or should I give in to civilized prejudice and cover my genitals? To see if I had enough material, I fashioned a rough diaper and decided right then to do the 'civilized' thing. It had nothing to do with modesty, but I discovered that protecting my vulnerables immediately gave me a sense of self-confidence that would be worth the price of sand-burred soles. Besides, I told myself, a sunburned cock would hurt far worse than sore feet.

I went to the well. An ancient stone affair, it didn't look like anyone had been near it in quite a while. Peeking over the rim I thought I could make out the glitter of water far below. Too far below. There wasn't any way I could get at it. I turned away reluctantly. At least Tamchakett was only forty kilometers away, I told myself soothingly. I should be able to make it in about twenty-four hours of fairly steady walking. Even supposing I didn't meet anyone along the way, I knew I could last that long without water. I was going to be mighty thirsty, but not dead (not yet, anyway, okay soul? I still have too much to do).

With a deep sigh and a pebble in my mouth I began plodding toward the fort. Benamar wasn't going to like this, I thought. I'd be lucky if I were merely declared *persona non grata* in Mauritania for the rest of my life. At worst, I might be placed in a Moorish prison while an investigation was carried out. Which could take several years. At best I might be able to sneak quietly up to the fort and get Jean-Pierre to fly me home before Benamar even knew I was back. He would want to fly after the Touaregs, but that wouldn't do any good. They would kill Darla and Salif and disappear before we could land, supposing we could find a place to land. If only the Chinese hadn't . . . The Chinese? Chu!

My plodding had taken me fifty yards when I remembered Chu. Maybe they had forgotten him. If so, he would still have clothes which I could wear after using them to make a line to get water. He might even have something I could use to make a canteen, like the flashlight case! I rushed back to where we had met on the path (rush being a purely relative concept at this point. I did move faster than a dung beetle). In more time than it takes to tell it, I had reached the spot. Chu was still there, minus most of his head. But he had been completely stripped. No sign of the flashlight, either.

Thoroughly pissed off at the efficiency of the raiders, I was about to return to my trek when my eye was caught by a bit of blueness at the edge of the path to the cave. I checked it out because *anything* might be useful in the state I was in. It was my passport. And lying next to it was the sack my okora had given me. They must have fallen out of my clothes when Maria was carrying them back to camp. I felt a flood of relief as I picked them up. The passport had no immediate survival value, but it was priceless in terms of future freedom. The fastest way to jail in Africa is to get picked up without a passport. When I got back to the fort and into Senegal it would be vital. What a lucky break! The sack I was less concerned with. I looked inside to see if there was anything useful, but it only contained three smooth, milky-white stones. I considered throwing them away and keeping the sack in case I found something to use it for, but the promise to my okora made me leave them in. Irrational, but what of it? So was life. Clutching the passport and the sack in my good hand, I returned to the trail.

The going wasn't too bad as long as the brush lasted. I stayed in shadows as much as possible and only breathed through my nose to cut down on evaporation. The help that gave was almost insignificant compared to what my bare body was letting escape, but where survival is concerned the tiniest things count a lot. Toward midday life became more hellish. Except for very scattered mesquite-type plants the brush was gone and the desert decor was all rocks and sand. In a way it would have been wiser just to travel at night. That would have doubled the time of the trip, however, and wouldn't have eased my thirst any. So I plodded on, building a rhythm of breathing and walking that would take my mind off the environment and the aches and pains of my body. Breathe in to the count of four steps, breathe out to the count of four steps, in for four, out for four, in for four, out for four. It was something like self-hypnotism. The sun was cooking my skin, my dangling arm was turning ugly colors, sand burrs were getting caught between my toes, and I was in a blank reverie with in for four, out for four, in for four, out for four. The whole day passed like that. Twilight came and went in the rapid desert way and I was walking by the light of the stars before I realized it. It didn't really matter, though. I couldn't stop. I had to keep up the rhythm and the walking. No attention to my skin or my arm. Just walk, walk, walk.

I walked for weeks, and then I walked for years, and on through the centuries I walked over hills and into forests fighting my way beyond castles and swimming across rivers that turned into oceans where I sailed on smooth waters to sweet-smelling islands and walked some more up tall mountains through snow-covered valleys and woke up with sand in my mouth.

Cautiously I opened my eyes. They gazed on a

miniature valley of blue-tinted sand that held a pellet of goat dung. I extended my awareness to see if the rest of my body was still there. It was. Stretched out full length on the ground with my toes still making walking motions. I stopped them. Gently, I moved my aching body to a sitting position. Sorry, body, I said to myself. I really put you through it, don't I? A nearly full moon was setting on one side of me and the sun was seriously considering coming up on the other. At least I had been walking in the right direction.

Suddenly my body told me it was cold. It communicated this important bit of information by shivering, which shook my arm and made it hurt, which made me swear. I didn't swear at my body because I was afraid it would get mad and stop working, but I swore at everything else. I swore as I got up still clutching my passport and the bag (I swore at them, too) and kept it up as I started walking again. I found that the swearing was making me feel better, even warmer, so I swore at everyone I had ever known, starting with my father. I went through my family and relatives and the hospital staff where I was born, and then took on my friends. I hit the men first, from Chuckie Rush in the second grade on up through Sami and Demba. Next I laid it on all my women, beginning with the little four-year-old chick who lured me into a hotel room when I was three to take my first puff of a cigarette, among other things (if you think three- and four-year-olds don't know anything about sex, you've led a sheltered life). The sun was riding high by the time I finished swearing at all my women. My enemies took the brunt of my swearing after that, and then I commenced swearing at everything I had ever done, all the good things, the bad things, the dumb and indifferent things. The sun was overhead when I ran out of things to swear at and I had hardly noticed the passage of time. It was good therapy. Apart from shooting pains in my arm, burning skin, sore feet and a headache, I felt great.

In a relatively happy state I looked around and cursed the sun, the sky, the sand, the heat. I swore at the ever-present dung balls and the stupid beetles who roll them around for a living. I gave it to the rocks and stones. I heard the bleating of a goat and I cussed that out, too. Wait a minute! A live goat? That meant...

A camel caravan was approaching from over a low ridge to my left. Thank God, whatever his name. The men on the lead camels were armed, but I could tell they were Moors. Behind them I could see a couple *khteir,* a sort of covered litter that the chief wives rode in. That told me for sure that it was a peaceful party. I stood where I was until the head man halted his camel beside me. *"Salaam alek,"* I croaked. He didn't answer me. He just held out his hand.

Puzzlement, disbelief, anger, shock. My emotional display of the next few minutes must have been something to behold. He was waiting for my okora's bag! Was it more than coincidence that the bag had been practically the only thing overlooked by the Touaregs? But if my okora could do that, why hadn't he helped me? Well, I was alive, wasn't I? And I had been met, hadn't I? My mind started to reel off into causality and probability and I cut if off short. Whoa, stop. I didn't want to think about it. My neatly ordered world (relatively speaking) was getting fuzzy. Back to the present moment. Ignore everything else. I had a bag. This man wanted the bag. He fit the description of the person I was supposed to give the bag to. So I gave him the bag.

Then things started to happen. The man on the camel tucked the bag in his shirt and shouted a whole string of orders. In moments, someone came forward to give me water, someone else began looking at my arm, others started setting up a tent. My memory of the rest is hazy except for the bright recall of two men holding my arm and snapping it back into place. Forgive me, but at that point I passed out.

I came to in an open-sided white cotton tent, lying on a green rug. As soon as I opened my eyes a boy seated near me yelled out and the head man came striding in.

"I am Abdul El Kerim, sheik of the Regueibat L'Gouassem," he said in Hassania as he sat down. "You are Leland Loring, an American from Dakar, adopted son of _____, and my brother." He reached over and clasped my hand in a way that let me know he was also a member of the secret society I had been initiated into. "How is your arm?"

"F-f-fine," I said in wonder. My broken arm was wrapped in something smelly with splints tied around it, and was in a sling. My tent scrap had been replaced with a white kaftan and my skin was covered with goo. But that wasn't the cause of the wonderment. I knew about the Regueibat. They were one of the largest tribes in Mauritania. They were almost pure Berber and ranged freely from Spanish Sahara to Timbuctu. Formerly feared warriors, they were now mostly marabouts, or religious leaders. The sheik was a very big cheese. To top it off, he not only knew the secret name of my okora, but was obviously a member of what I had thought was just a local religious organization. I began to get a sinking feeling that I was involved in something way over my head. And for an ego like mine, that's hard to admit.

"The poultice on your arm and the ointment on your skin should help to heal you very quickly. They had better, for you will need all your strength on your journey."

"What journey..." But he held up his hand and tilted his head as if listening for something. Seconds later a man came running up to the tent.

"A Land Rover, from Tamchakett!"

"Go stop it and bring the occupants here," ordered my host.

I could hear it now, roaring toward us. In a few minutes Benamar made his appearance at the tent. "Welcome, *commandant*," said El Kerim. "We are about to have some tea. Won't you join us?"

"With pleasure," grunted Benamar as he sat beside me. "Greetings, Loring." He glanced at my arm. "And what trouble have you gotten yourself into now?"

"I don't know, yet, but I think it's bad." Then I told him everything that had happened at the camp.

Benamar stared horrified while I spoke. When I finished he wiped a hand over his face and said, "I'm afraid I'm going to have to arrest you, my friend, until we find what this is all about. Come, we'll have to go to the camp first to check your story." He made as if to rise, but El Kerim stopped him with a gentle hand on his shoulder.

El Kerim's voice was soft, but commanding. "The tea is arriving and there is much to talk about. This is not just a matter for government bureaucracy, as you will see." A boy came in with the tea and served it. El Kerim went on, "I think I will tell you a story. Then perhaps you will understand.

"About a thousand years ago, in the early days of the Empire of Ghana, there lived a marvelous woodcarver. It was said that if he carved the likeness of a bird it would sing; and that if he carved an antelope it would bound away before anyone could catch it. People came from all over the world, it is said, just to see his work. Very, very few ever left with a sample of it, however, because the Emperor was extremely jealous. Nearly everything the woodcarver made he took for himself and locked it up in a well-guarded fortress. One day, so the story goes, the woodcarver was working in his yard all alone as storm clouds gathered in the sky. The rumbling of thunder didn't disturb him, nor did the scattered raindrops. He was absorbed in his carving and barely aware of anything else.

"Suddenly a bolt of lightning struck an ebony tree in the woodcarver's yard, splitting it in half. The woodcarver looked up in time to see a block of wood from the heart of the tree tumble out and land at his feet. Now, some would say that what happened next was only the result of shock and the sound of thunder, but the woodcarver, says the story, saw a great light where the tree was split and heard a terrible voice speak directly to him. 'Take this block of wood,' said the voice, 'and carve from it a mask. Glorify it with silver from the West, gold from the South, precious stones from the East and amber from the North. Carve it and decorate it according to the vision I show you now.' Then the woodcarver saw a vision so beautiful and so terrifying that he cried out and covered his eyes. 'You have seen the Face of God,' continued the voice, 'and you shall not forget it. After you have finished the likeness, take it away from this land. Gather men around you to protect it and form from them a secret society to help the weak and fight oppression. All those who pledge service to the Face of God shall instantly obey the guardian of the mask. Whosoever wears the mask with a pure heart shall see the world as it really is and be a streambed for power seldom given mortal men. But a hundred deaths await the wearer with a dark heart. Therefore, wear it seldom and guard it well.'

"With that, the voice and the light disappeared. The woodcarver picked up the block of wood, which seemed to tremble in his hands, and did as he was told. Over the centuries the society grew and grew and did its work in silence. Then one day a man of dark heart killed the guardian of the mask and put it on. He died in a manner I do not wish to describe, but his followers took the mask and sold it. It has since been lost. The society seeks it dilligently, but fears its reappearance in other hands. For although the wisest of the members will follow their own minds, there are many others who will obey the mask's keeper, whoever it is." El Kerim stopped his narrative.

I kept quiet. I remembered my okora's mention of the Face of God, and now I thought I knew what had been in that canvas bag that made me tingle.

Benamar smiled indulgently. "A nice story, El Kerim, and well told. However, I fail to see the connection with Loring and with the disaster that just took place."

"The connection is straightforward, *commandant*. Loring is a member of that society. The real purpose of the archeological expedition was to retrieve the mask which had probably been hidden near the site. Loring has been chosen to get the mask back, and the task will not be easy."

I wanted to cry out, Not me, brother! But something told me to keep my trap shut.

The *commandant* was dumbfounded. "Are you trying to tell me that story was true? That there is such a mask and such a society? I don't believe it! For one thing, there is no God but Allah, and no likeness can be made of his image. Your story was entertaining, but only a tale for children."

It was El Kerim's turn to smile. "Of course, every good follower of Islam knows that Allah's image, blessed be his name, cannot be carved. But that is not the point, you see. What matters is that so many *believe* in the power of the mask. If it should fall into the hands of the Chinese Secret Service or the CIA, for instance, they could use it to stimulate terrorism and revolution throughout the continent for their own political ends. Revolution and terrorism will occur anyway, but I wish to emphasize that to use the mask in such a way would result in destruction on such a scale that you cannot imagine it!"

Benamar fidgeted. "El Kerim, I have the greatest respect for you. Your story is not... well, let us say that it stretches the bounds of credibility. I have to deal with the practical effects of the moment, however. There has been looting and murder in the territory under my jurisdiction, and I have here the one witness to it all. There has even been a kidnapping of foreigners. The international repercussions are serious. Since I am not exactly in the President's favor at the moment, this could either be a chance to regain favor or it could mean my imprisonment, depending on how I handle it. You seem to be proposing that I let Loring go, which leaves the whole thing on my shoulders. I'm sorry, but I'm not going to allow that."

"What I propose is more than that, *commandant*. I propose that the incident never happened."

"What!"

"What!" The first 'what' was Benamar's. The second was mine.

"I propose that the Chinese doctor and his assistant got lost in the desert on their way to Nouakchott. That is not implausible, since they did not have a guide with them. I also propose that the archeological expedition finished its work and headed for some smaller ruins to the north, near Tichitt. They, too, got lost, and both parties no doubt died of thirst. No one expects to hear from them for three weeks, anyway. The regrettable incidents take place weeks apart. The great Sahara has simply claimed more victims."

"What about the remains of the fire that Loring described?"

"My men will take care of removing all trace of it. The vehicles will be buried. We had received word that Touregs had chased local tribes from the area, threatening them with death if they told the authorities, and we were on our way to Aoudaghost with sufficient men to deal with the raiders. Unfortunately we arrived too late, but we still have enough men to clean up the area in one day."

"My soldiers will know."

"No, you will leave them here to ask my men questions about conditions in the desert. Then you and my brother, who is driver, will go on to Aoudaghost. There you can check the situation and tell my brother what needs to be done."

"What of Loring's pilot, the Frenchman?"

"You will bring him a note from Loring telling him to return to Dakar until further word."

"You know, Sheik Abdul El Kerim," laughed Benamar, "I almost get the feeling that this whole thing has been planned and staged by you."

"I would rather say that Allah, in his great wisdom, has permitted me to see these circumstances as among the possibilities of life."

"Praise Allah! I am beginning to believe that this might work."

"It will work. I will even arrange to have tribesmen report to you that they have seen the Chinese to the west and the expedition to the north on their way to their destinations. You will have no incident to worry about."

"I can see that, and I'm grateful. Now we are only

left with two problems. I do not consider the mask to be my problem. The other two are the fact that two persons have been kidnapped and may yet be murdered, and the fact that Loring here is at liberty."

"I don't see that as a problem, personally," I piped up. "Instead of sending a note to Jean-Pierre, I'll go back to Tamchakett and we'll fly back to Dakar. The expedition can get 'lost' after my departure and I'll arrange a plane search. Meanwhile, the sheik could have some of his men track the Touaregs and..."

El Kerim interrupted me. "That cannot be, my brother. Life is much like the desert. There are many trails that lead to the same place. Some of these trails are more difficult than others, some have sure death and disappointment along them, others have the possibility of success. Through the grace of Allah I have looked along the trails that lead to recovery of the mask and the one where death and failure is least certain is the one where you trod the path."

"In other words, you want *me* to track down experienced Touaregs into the Sahara, fight them plus Russian agents, and save Darla, Salif and the mask?"

"Yes. But not alone. I will send my brother's son with you."

"Terrific! What do you think this is, a movie? I'm broken in limb and worn down in spirit and you think I'm going to rush off into the desert like Lawrence of Arabia or something. No thanks. A dead hero I'd rather not be."

"It is the only way to save your friends and the mask."

"Camelshit!" I was standing now, angry because I

felt I was being set up. "Will Allah guarantee that for me, in writing?"

"Nothing is guaranteed in this life. It is always possible that you will fail, but there is less possibility if you go than if we try any other way."

"I don't buy that! It makes no sense to send a cripple and a boy out after three times their number of killers. Why do you want me out of the way? Why not just kill me and bury me here? It would be a lot easier."

"It is not written that life should make sense. I only tell you what I have seen."

"Seen where? In a crystal ball? I'd rather you told me I was going to meet a tall, dark woman..." I suddenly thought of Maria. "No, skip that. I refuse to act stupid on advice from a fortune-teller."

"Allah does grant me visions of what can be. However, men make their own fortunes within the bounds of his will." His voice took on a colder tone. "Allah has also given me the power to make cruel decisions when I have to. You are going, Loring. It is now only a question of what inducement to use to get you to make the choice yourself. I can call upon the oath you took when you joined the society, I can call upon your love for your friends who will surely die if you do not go, or I can turn you over to the *commandant* who will charge you with murder and see that you spend many safe and secure years in prison. Would you not cooperate, *Commandant*"

"Anything for a friend."

"That's not fair!" I shouted.

"Nor is it written that life should be fair. I sense that you have made your choice." He rose to his feet, and Benamar with him. "Stay here, Loring. I will send men to help you make preparations. It is important that you leave before sunset. Come, *Commandant,* my brother is waiting to take you to Aoudaghost."

Benamar paused, and took my hand. "You have a knack for getting into trouble, my friend. I think that secretly you look for it. Your only choice now is to have faith in the sheik. Peace, and Allah's protection go with you." They left.

"And with you, peace," I sighed dejectedly. Trouble wasn't my middle name, I decided. It was my *first* name.

Preparations didn't take long. I was fitted out with a loose cotton shirt and the blue ankle-length bloomers affected by the nomads. Over that went a light wool burnoose and a turban was wrapped around my head. Thin leather sandals and a dagger completed my costume. Oh, there was a rifle, too. A .30-06 Springfield with a bandolier of ammunition. How I was supposed to fire it with only one arm, I didn't know. I felt more like Lawrence every minute.

All too soon it was time to go. The riding camels were saddled and a baggage camel was loaded with guerbas and camping gear. I was mounted and the sheik's seventeen-year-old nephew, Daoud, was ready next to me. El Kerim came up to give us a few parting words of encouragement.

"I'm not sure you'll make it. The way is long and hard and you are still not healed. And Daoud, though experienced in the desert, has never fought in a battle. Yet this is nonetheless better than other plans whose outcome would surely be failure. At least in this there is a chance of success."

"Thanks loads. That really makes me feel good."

"You are not happy about it, I know, but I ask you to have faith."

"I don't have much choice, do I?"

"Oh, you have many choices. It is just that they all seem less pleasing than this one."

"This is a lousy time for philosophy. Don't you have anything more practical to say before I go off to tilt my windmills?"

"Windmills? Ah yes, don Quixote. I just hope the windmills you find have a bad aim. The Touareg probably did not head north for more than a day's march. They must be on their way east now, heading for Timbuctu. That will be a three or four week journey. The village of Oualata lies along their route but they will avoid it because of the police post. A half day's march north of the village is the well of Charaioun, used only rarely nowadays. I suspect they will stop there for a night. Daoud knows the place. You can reprovision at Oualata and pick up their trail at the well."

"That sounds nice, but how in a djinn's name am I supposed to pick up a trail in the desert? The wind will cover all their traces. I could be a couple miles to one side of them and never know it."

"The mask will guide you."

I made a face. "Let's leave the Arabian Nights stuff out of this, okay? It's bad enough that I have to risk my life because of your visions. A magical mask would be just too much."

"Did you not say that you felt a tingling or a

prickling whenever you were near the mask?"

"Well, yes, but that was just something like static electricity."

"Call it what you like. What is static electricity, after all? The point is that you felt something from the mask. On the trail, whenever you are in doubt about the direction to take, compose yourself in silence as your okora taught you and you will feel the same sensation in a part of your body facing the direction of the mask."

"All my problems are solved. What if I tune in a power line?"

"There are no power lines in that part of the Sahara."

"Sorry, poor joke. Look, just supposing we do make it and I get the mask back..." here I had to pause while a bit of hysterical laughter welled up and out of me... "what am I supposed to do with it?"

"When that time comes you will know."

"Ah, *merde mille fois*! I am really getting sick of all this supernatural mystery you keep throwing in. Why can't you give me straight facts?" If he handed me a lantern to rub I was ready to bust him with it.

"What you call a fact, friend Loring, is only an experience that fits a preconceived notion. There is nothing supernatural because Allah made all, and therefore all that is is natural. However, you are not yet aware of all that is, and certain parts of Allah's creation are still strange to you. It is a fact—a circumstance that will take place as surely as the sun will rise tomorrow—that when you have the mask you will know what to do with it. You would like to know how and why, but who can describe a cloud to a blind man? It will just happen, if it is Allah's will that the sun shall rise again."

I gave up. El Kerim would have made a great encyclopedia salesman. "Sheik Abdul, much as I enjoy life I don't expect to have it last too long. I'm forced to go on this chase, regardless of what you say about choices, that's how I feel, and I can't honestly see how I can make it all the way to Timbuctu in the shape I'm in, short of a miracle. And you've as much as said that they don't exist, so I guess that's the end of it. At least do me the favor of letting my friend Demba N'Diaye in Dakar know what's up so he can take care of my affairs and execute my will."

"I will let him know where you are and what you do. And do not speak of dying before you are dead, my brother. You will win through and have the praise of all of Africa."

"Seriously, I'd rather have a cold beer. Peace, brother. Ready, Daoud?" I took the little stick that served as a combination riding crop and goad and rapped my camel with it. *"Ayyoua!"* I shouted. "Giddap!"

8/Dakar

Let's shift the scene back to Dakar. Three days before I was about to launch my ship of the desert into the Saharan sea, Sami and his sons and Aletha and friends had set out for N'Gor to save me from the dastardly clutches of somebody or other because of the false tip given by Darla. The island isn't very large, so it didn't take them more than an hour and a half to realize I wasn't being held in any of the cabins. Leaving behind some outraged Frenchmen and embarrassed PAN AM stewardesses, they rushed back across the bay to be met by a messenger from my okora who told them I was safe and sound and on my way to Tamchakett. Thus relieved, they headed for their respective domiciles. Early the next morning, Sami got Aliberti and Benedetti to the airport where Jean-Pierre was waiting with Darla. Sami had heard about Darla but had never met her, so he had no objections to make about J-P taking an American tourist along for the ride. Maria's protests were ignored.

Demba, meanwhile, had spent an ecstatic night in Rokhaya's room at the N'Gor Hotel. He was exhaustedly asleep when Darla slipped in to let Rocky know of the change in plans. During Darla's absence, Rocky's job would be to keep Demba distracted and in Dakar. It sounded like a cinch, but the best laid plans of mice and women often get shaken up, to misquote a famous Scot.

The sun was an hour above the horizon when Demba woke up to answer a call of nature. On his way back to bed he stopped to gaze at Rokhaya, apparently still asleep. In their love struggles they had thrown back all the covers and Rokhaya lay there now on the single sheet, bare and beautiful. She lay partly on her side, with one leg drawn up. Half an arm was hidden under a pillow, the other rested lightly across her waist. Sunlight touched a shoulder and a hip, and a coolish breeze from the open windows reminded Demba of some lines from Senghor's poem, *Femme Noire,* that he murmured softly:

> "Naked woman, dark woman
> Firm skin like ripe fruit, shadowy ecstasy of black wine,
> mouth that makes my mouth sing
> Like a field with clear horizons, a field that trembles to the fervent caress of the Eastern Wind..."

Rokhaya moved, stretched, opened her eyes and held out her arms. "Demba, come."

Desire spread through him like an autumn fire. A brief thought that he shouldn't let himself be controlled by this instant lust flickered and was swept away as he moved toward her. In a moment she was below him, her mouth and breasts and loins fanning the flame. And the phone rang.

It rang too long to be ignored, so Demba rolled aside, a little dizzy at being brought back so quickly from the heights of passion, as Rocky answered the call. "Hello? No, he isn't here. What? Oh. All right. Here he is." She sighed. "It's for you. Your office. I wish you hadn't trained your men so well."

Demba grinned and took the receiver. "N'Diaye. When? How many? I'll be right there." He hung up and reluctantly got out of bed. "There was a fight of some kind by Loring's office. The police found two dead bodies and a man with a broken collarbone. Apparently they got into his office. Loring was supposed to take off for Mauritania this morning. Why don't you call Darla and see if he made it."

"There's no need. Darla left with the archeologists, but Loring is missing."

"What! How do you know that?"

"Darla came in early this morning while you were asleep. She and Lee had some trouble on the way to the airport..."

"I shouldn't have let you talk me into taking the other route!"

"... but they got out of it okay. He let her off at the hotel and went home. When she tried to get in touch with him later, she couldn't find him anywhere. However, she called me from the airport just before the plane took off—you didn't even budge when the phone rang—and told me that Lee's Lebanese friend said he would meet them in Tamchakett. He's probably there now."

"Maybe. I want to make certain of that."

Rocky came up behind Demba as he was buttoning his shirt and put her arms around him. "Are you really sorry that we came back to the hotel by ourselves last night?" Her hands caressed his chest.

"Don't try to confuse me. I'm not sorry about what we did, but I'll be sorry if Lee's in trouble."

She pressed her body to his and kissed his neck. "I'll be sorry if you're angry with me."

"I'm not angry." Demba tried to finish buttoning his shirt but his fingers forgot what they were doing as Rocky's hands moved over his stomach and played with his belt. With a sense of helplessness he turned and took her in his arms. "Rokhaya," he mumbled, "I want you so much."

Rocky melted against him and raised his lust level to a few notches short of the breaking point, then gently pushed away. "And I want you, my mountain of a man, but first we have to check on our friend. I'll go with you to his office. I'm as concerned about Lee as you are." Her job was to distract Demba, and she well knew that nothing distracts a man like unsatisfied sex.

A little weak-kneed, Demba finally got his shirt buttoned and watched as Rocky dressed. When she was ready he very nearly decided to take her clothes off again, but she managed to get him down to the car.

By the time they got to Loring's office the police had gone, taking the bodies with them. Aletha was sitting forlornly at her desk and one of Demba's men, Bocar, was standing by. When Aletha saw them she ran up to Demba and took his hands. "Oh, Demba, I'm so glad you're here. It's been an awful night. First I got a call saying that Lee was kidnapped and we couldn't find him and then a man told Sami that he was all right and then I came to work and found the office broken into and bodies lying around and now I'm afraid that Lee's in serious trouble and I don't know what to do!"

"Hey, 'Letha, it's okay. Loring knows how to take care of himself. I'm sure he's safe. Maybe those guys were just thieves and he messed them up on his way out. Was anything stolen?"

Bocar answered. "Doesn't seem like it. A few art pieces were broken, apparently during the fight. The door was open when Aletha got here and the injured man was inside in a faint. The other two were in the hall."

"Demba, Lee wouldn't have someone inside with the door open."

"I know, 'Letha. At least, not unless he was in an awful hurry."

Aletha was back at her desk and now seemed to notice Rokhaya for the first time. "Aren't you a friend of Darla Moore?" Her tone had a tinge of suspicion about it.

"Sorry," said Demba. "This is Rokhaya Fall. Friend of mine. And of Darla's. Friend of Lee's, too."

"Is Darla mixed up in this? She was here the other

day. I don't care who Lee wastes his time with, but if she had anything to do with his disappearance..." Aletha was getting back up and there was fire in her eyes.

"Pull your claws back in, *cherie*," Rocky said coolly. "Darla's away on a trip. We all want to know what happened to Lee as badly as you do."

Aletha looked soothed, so Demba figured it was prudent not to add that Darla's trip was to the same place Loring was supposed to be going. "Bocar," he said, "I want a man down at the station where they're holding the live one to see what info he can pick up. Wait. 'Letha, is it okay if we say you've hired us to investigate the break-in?"

"Of course."

"Good. Okay, Bocar, keep someone on my private line and I'll be in touch later. Right now I'm going over to see Sami."

"Done. Oh, by the way, I have two messages for you. One's from Sami, he wants to see you right away. The other's from Allen Crawford. He'd like to see you at his office at two, if you can make it."

"Crawford? Wonder what he wants? Probably some more petty information on a scandal among the diplomats." To himself he wondered if it had anything to do with Lee. Officially, Crawford was a flunky attached to the Political Section of the U.S. Embassy, but virtually everyone knew he was the up front CIA man. The U.S. almost always had one man who was well known to be with the CIA. This supposedly allowed him to take the brunt of surveillance and give the "quiet" operatives more freedom. Nevertheless, he sometimes had good information to trade. "Tell him I'll meet him. Maybe

I can pick up some good stuff myself. Aletha, don't worry about Lee. We'll find him. If we get any news I'll let you know. And if you get any news, call my office. Okay?"

"Okay, Demba. Thanks."

A few minutes later, Demba and Rocky were entering Sami's digs. The knotty pine and the forest scene were still in effect. Sami, however, looked very unhappy. He looked even unhappier after Rokhaya was introduced as a friend of Darla's.

"Are you sure you want her here, Demba? Lee's in enough trouble."

"She's okay, Sami. She's working with me. Go ahead. What's the trouble?"

Sami gave a resigned sigh. "Well, to begin with, right after the wild chase on N'Gor a boy brought me a message from someone named a Baba N'Dow saying that Lee was okay and on his way to Mauritania. I took it at face value at the time, but since I heard about the break-in at his office I'm beginning to have doubts. Do you know who N'Dow might be?"

Demba shook his head. "No one I can think of."

"I know of Baba N'Dow." Rokhaya spoke in an odd voice. "He's a Lebou sorcerer."

"Do you know where he is?" asked Demba.

"I know *of* him. I've heard of him. He's one of those who never accepted Islam. From what I've heard he maintains the ancient traditions and has quite a few followers scattered around. I've never met him, though."

"Is there any reason to believe that Lee might know him?"

"Who can say? We all know he's interested in that

kind of thing."

"It doesn't do any good to speculate on who he might be," said Sami, "unless we know where to find him. Can either of you help with that?" Not receiving any response, Sami went on. "Then on with the bad news. Lee asked me to do further checking on those archeologists. No problem with the old man. He's legit. Benedetti's another matter. I got a call from Italy early this morning. The real Maria Benedetti was located in a hospital at a little ski resort in the Alps. If she hadn't broken her leg we might never have found this out. Seems she was being paid a pretty penny to hide out up there while someone else used her passport. I guess even the wealthy can be bought. Intellectuals, too. Aliberti pretended his companion was Benedetti in return for the financing of this trip."

"Then who was the girl who came with him?"

"Don't know that, yet. Not her name, anyway. What we do know is that she's a Russian agent. The Soviets are the ones who paid out the money."

"*Mbas!* They're probably the ones who've been setting Lee up to be killed."

"Probably. I imagine they just wanted to use him to get into Mauritania. It would be too inconvenient to have him go along. So now, supposing he made it, Lee has a spy on his hands just waiting to get rid of him as soon as his back is turned. What I can't figure is what interest they have in Aoudaghost. It must be something important for all the effort they've put into it."

"Considering what he's gone through, I think Lee will be on his toes."

"He's more likely to be on his elbows. That agent is a very beautiful woman. Much as I respect our friend, his brain does tend to get a little hazy around beauty, especially when there's no one around to straighten him out. He needs help and he doesn't have it."

"He does have some help, Sami." Rocky, who had been quiet, now spoke up. "Darla went to Mauritania, too."

"When was that?"

"This morning, on the plane with the archeologists."

"That dumb redhead was Darla?"

"Appearances only, Sami. The hair is real, but she isn't dumb. If anyone can help Lee, she can."

"*Mon Dieu*! I can't help feeling he's worse off with her than without her. From what I've heard she's as likely to get rid of him as the other one."

"This time she's under orders to help. With Darla on the job you can be sure Lee will be safe."

"I'll keep my doubts, just the same."

"What now? Should one of us go to Mauritania?"

"I don't think so, Demba. In the first place, we don't know for sure that Lee's there. In the second place, they won't let me in and it would take you a week to get a visa while they argued about letting a detective go. Salif is there and if Lee doesn't show within a reasonable time he'll get a message back. Hopefully, Lee will get a message back if he makes it."

"Well, if we have to wait here we might as well make the best of it. I'll see what I can dig up on why everyone is in such an uproar about Aoudaghost."

"And I'll see what I can find out in Italy and elsewhere." Sami leaned back thoughtfully. "You know, it's an odd feeling not knowing what's going on in your own territory. It's like a jockey without a horse watching a race on his home turf. He can see the action, but can't take part even though he knows the track. I intend to get me a horse."

"It might be safer on the sidelines, Sami. That way there's nothing to lose." Demba and Rocky were at the door.

Sami got up to let them out. "Maybe, but if you don't race you can't win, either. Nice meeting you, Rokhaya. Keep in touch, Demba. *Ciao.*"

It was after eleven, so Demba took Rocky for a leisurely lunch at the restaurant of the *Hotel de L'Independance,* where the *hors-d'ouevres variees* are outstanding and the meat is flown in daily from France. Afterward he sent her home in a taxi with a promise to pick her up at seven for dinner. Then he walked to the U.S. Embassy for his meeting with Crawford.

"Come in, Mr. N'Diaye. Glad you could come. Have a seat." Allen Crawford was behind his desk in a smallish room with maps of Senegal and Africa on the walls and a bulletin board full of administrative notices. He was a tall man with sandy hair and glasses and an open, friendly smile. He rose slightly to shake Demba's hand.

"All right, Mr. Crawford, what can I do for you?"

"Maybe we can do something for each other, Mr. N'Diaye. The Ambassador likes me to keep on top of current affairs in Senegal and I thought you might be able to help me confirm a rumor that's going about."

"What kind of rumor?"

"Oh, just a minor thing. More cultural than political, really. I know that most Senegalese are Moslem, but there are still a lot who cling to pagan traditions, aren't there?"

"If you mean pre-Christian and pre-Islamic, yes, of course. Everyone knows that."

"Well, is it still very strong? I mean in terms of dedication to such beliefs."

"What do you mean by dedication? Even Moslem Ouolofs, many of them, still believe in ghosts and the evil eye and wear fetishes. Some peoples worship nature spirits and in the Casamance there's a village that worships a crocodile. So what?"

"I guess what I'm trying to ask is whether it's very organized."

"Mr. Crawford, are you talking about secret societies?"

"Yes, I suppose you could say that."

This was taking a strange turn, thought Demba. "Maybe you'd better tell me what the rumor is, first."

Crawford lit a cigarette and took a few puffs before answering. "The rumor is that there is a certain restlessness among a particular secret society with branches in several countries because of some object that was stolen from them. I just wondered if they had a branch here."

"Most of such societies in Senegal are local and strictly religious, or religious and economic. There are the Moslem Brotherhoods, of course, but you could hardly call them secret, or pagan."

"The one I'm interested in is supposed to be secret and pagan, although I wouldn't be surprised if it has some Christian and Moslem members. I don't know its Senegalese name, or even if there is a Senagalese branch, but its name in Mali is *Arjunate.* Do you know of it?"

"Never heard of it before." Which wasn't strictly true. Demba hadn't heard of that particular name, which was a Bambara word, but he knew that it meant "Followers of the Face of God." That he had heard of, since he had an uncle and a cousin who belonged to it. He knew nothing about their practices, however, and wasn't aware that they were restless. In any case, he had no right to mention anything about it. "Just how restless are they supposed to be?"

"Oh, enough to commit acts of terrorism, which could be upsetting to an insecure government. Haven't heard that anything has actually happened, but there are rumors that it might. If you hear of any restlessness in Senegal I'd be very appreciative if you'd let me know. Very appreciative."

Demba laughed loudly. "Mr. Crawford, Senegal has a very secure government, no terrorism and no 'restless natives.' If you want to know more about secret societies, though, I'd suggest you go see Amadou Seck at the University. He's a professor of history and a specialist in Pre-Islamic Traditions. He can tell you a lot more than I can."

"Why thank you, Mr. N'Diaye." He quickly wrote down the name. "Now maybe I can do you a favor. You're a friend of Lee Loring, the art dealer, aren't you?"

"That's right." The tone was casual, but Demba was suddenly very attentive.

"I hear he's been missing since last night and that there was some kind of ruckus at his office."

"My, how news does travel. What's the favor?"

"I've also heard that he was seen in the Medina last night looking for a man named... uh, let's see now..." he checked a scrap of notepaper "... Baba N'Dow, apparently a very mysterious personage. Can't get any information on him at all. Does the name mean anything at all to you?"

"Not a thing," Demba lied, "but I'll check it out." Demba decided that Crawford might be useful in the future, so he set up an information debt account. "By the way, did you decorate this office yourself?"

Crawford looked startled. "No, it was like this when I got here. Why?"

"Just that we sometimes have a problem with spiders in these old buildings and they like to hide under maps because no one ever bothers to move them. You could get a nasty bite." Demba could tell from the look in Crawford's eyes that he understood Demba was talking about a "bug."

"Thank you again, Mr. N'Diaye. I'll have someone check it out. Is there anything else I can do for you?"

"No thanks. See you around." They shook hands and Demba left. His mind was full of questions now. Who was Baba N'Dow? Was he the Lebou sorcerer that Rokhaya mentioned? Why had Loring gone to see him? Where could he be found? He'd have to get his staff on it. Why did Lee always have to get in so much trouble?

Demba called his office from a hotel phone and was told that the guy with the broken collarbone had said that he and his pals were waiting for Loring when they were attacked by four men and a toubab woman who fought like a devil. The effort of getting that much out of him had rendered him unconscious and he was still out. Demba told them to find out what they could about Baba N'Dow, and he'd call back at seven. Then he headed for his car, thinking about the "toubab woman." Who else could that be but Darla? What was she trying to do leading a gang against another gang waiting to cream Lee? Protect him? But she didn't even know what happened to him, according to Rokhaya. What a mess!

He was just getting into his car when a beggar approached, a leper with a twisted face and no fingers on his outstretched hand. Demba dropped a twenty-five franc piece into his palm and started to shut the door.

"Diar dieff!" The beggar cried his thanks, deftly flipped the coin into a pocket of his ragged boubou, and tapped Demba on the shoulder.

"What is it? That's all you're going to get."

"No more money, brother. I was told to give you this message: Rokhaya Fall is waiting for you at the abandoned cigarette factory on the *Route de Rufisque*. She needs your help."

Ordinarily, Demba would have questioned the man to find out who gave him the message, and then he would have called the hotel to see if Rocky was still there. But this time his concern overrode his caution. He gave the beggar a hundred francs and tore off in the direction of the factory. Along the way he could only think that Rocky was in trouble and he had to help her.

Fifteen minutes later he was on the grounds of the abandoned enterprise. The cigarette factory was well away from the other industries that lined the route and an abundance of weeds had grown up around it. All the windows and doors in the front were boarded up, so he went around to the back. Now he moved with caution. In the center of the back wall was a metal door. Demba walked slowly up and tried the catch. It was open. He pushed it inward a few inches.

"Rocky? Rokhaya! Are you in there?" No sound. With his foot he shoved the door all the way open. The bright sun outside made the interior impenetrably black. "Rocky?" This time he definitely heard a muffled whimper. All his experience warned him that it was probably a trap, but he had to make the best of it. With a wild cry he made a running dive into the opening.

He heard a swishing sound past his head before he crashed into a chair and bumped hard against somebody's legs. As he rammed a fist into that person's crotch he caught a glimpse of two men by the doorway in momentary confusion. They moved toward him and Demba scrambled to his feet with the remains of the chair in one hand. He smashed the chair into one man's face and sidestepped to avoid the pipe being swung by the other. A thick arm circled his throat from behind. He ducked and threw the man over his head, but another swing from the pipe got him on the shoulder and spun him around in time to meet a heavy fist in his solar plexus. He collapsed to his knees and a foot struck him in the face, knocking him backward. He managed to roll over and miss getting a block of wood between the eyes, but as he tried to rise the pipe slammed into his kidneys, another foot kicked him in the chest and something else hit him on the head. At that point he blacked out.

When he finally woke up he wished he hadn't. His body felt like it was on fire in a million places. Only one eye was working, and he knew the other must be swollen shut. Then he became aware that he was standing up, and stark naked. His arms were tied behind him and forced up, probably attached to a rafter overhead, and ropes were tied to his ankles, forcing them well apart. In front of him he could see three Africans sitting on the floor, playing cards. One of them had a bloody head. A second looked at Demba and said, "He's awake." The third man stood up, grimaced as he clutched his crotch, and said, "Now I'm going to kill him!"

From behind Demba a harsh voice ordered, "Not yet. He must talk to me first..." The voice spoke Wolof, but with a terrible accent. "Now, tell me, N'Diaye, where is Leland Loring?"

Demba wanted to laugh, but he couldn't. All he could do was grunt and say, "I don't know. Can't find him myself."

Apparently a signal was given, because the man who had first noticed that Demba was awake picked up a length of rubber hose and came and stood before him. Without warning he swung the hose upward and Demba felt a flash of agony throughout his groin. Twice more the hose slashed upward, leaving Demba with bile in his mouth and cold sweat on his body. He might have screamed, but pain was all he knew for sure.

"Where is Loring?" The voice sifted through the clouds of hurt.

Tell him something. Anything! Got to stop that hose. "Uh, he's hiding out, at his place on Goree. Waiting till dark."

"False. His place on Goree has been watched."

"Aaaaaaaahhhhhh!" Up came the hose again. Vomit flowed over Demba's chest. Everything hurt. Have to tell the truth. "Went... went to Kaolack. Took a plane to Mauritania," he gasped. "'Swhat I was told."

"False. All the roads to Kaolack have been watched. You are being uselessly stubborn."

Damn his soul, thought Demba. What does he want to hear? For the third time the hose whipped in short sets against him. There was no more thinking. Only blinding whiteness, and then utter dark.

"We will wait," said the voice. "He will awaken again. And he will be much more tender."

Seven thirty ticked its way into the past and Rokhaya began to worry. She called Demba's office, but he hadn't checked in. They weren't concerned because that happened frequently. "No cause for alarm," Bocar had said. "He's probably having a drink with a source." Rocky could hardly tell him that she knew Demba wouldn't let that delay him from getting her back in bed. It wasn't ego on her part. She simply knew her man and the effect she had on him. What added to her worry was the telephone conversation she had with Circe. Using coded gossip she had learned that an international hunt was on for a mask known as the "Face of God" which had been stolen from a powerful secret society. According to the available information, whoever held the mask could control the society. That could lead to unlimited possibilities for political intrigue and espionage. It was in the interest of the Lorelei to obtain the mask and the new assignment for Rokhaya and Darla was to get it. So far the secret services of Red China, Russian, France and the U.S. were all trying to get their hands on it. The British were still in the dark and, strangely enough, the African governments didn't seem to give it any importance. Loring was thought to be an agent of the CIA. That and his knowledge of art were what made him seem so dangerous to others. Darla and Rocky were to work with Loring and his friends until the mask was found. Then they were to take it.

By eight o'clock Rocky was convinced that Demba was delayed against his will. Quite apart from her personal feelings, she now had an obligation to help him as a friend of Loring involved in the hunt for the mask. If it weren't for that fact she knew she would abandon him. With regret, perhaps, but without hesitation. However, in the present situation her duties and desires happened to match.

Find Demba. The question was where to look? His staff didn't know. He had met with Crawford. Maybe that was a clue. She called Crawford's home. From the background sounds she could tell he was giving a party. No, he didn't know the whereabouts of Mr. N'Diaye. They had talked for a half hour and then he left. Sorry he couldn't help her further. What did she say her name was? Rocky hung up and thought some more. He could have tried to check on Lee's contacts with the African traders. Who would know them best? Aletha. She called Aletha and got her at home. Demba was missing and she had some ideas on how to find Lee, she told Aletha. Could she come over? Good, she'd be right there.

There was no telling what might happen, so Rocky donned a black leotard before putting on her colorful African dress and boubou. A special strap around her thigh held three throwing knives and under her left breast was a pocket containing a very lightweight and exceedingly flat .22 automatic. Not much later she was standing in front of Aletha's apartment house on Avenue Roume. It was a new building, with a locked gate and an outside intercom so the inhabitants would know who they were letting in. Rocky pressed the buzzer for Aletha's apartment. When the connection was made she said, "This is Rokhaya Fall." Aletha said she would be right down.

Now, coincidence is a marvelous thing. To some it implies a chance happening, the temporal juxtaposition of two unrelated events. To others, however, all events are related. For them, when two events take place simultaneously it is like the crossing of two lines in a pattern. Life is full of such crossings, but probably the only thing that matters is how we react to them.

As Rocky spoke her name into the intercom she didn't notice the leprous beggar passing by on the sidewalk. Ordinarily, he wouldn't have paid any attention to her, either, in spite of the fact that he had heard her name before and had even spoken it, for Wolof women were not usually generous to beggars. But this one was a little more intelligent—or larcenous—than others, and so he changed his direction and went up to her.

"Your name is Rokhaya Fall?" he asked.

"Yes," she said impatiently, expecting a plea for alms.

"Do you know a tall man with broad shoulders, looking like a proper N'Diaye, and who drives a black Peugeot?"

Rocky whirled around and narrowed her eyes. "I do. What do you know about him?"

The beggar backed away. There was something fearful about this woman. Still, the opportunity to make a few francs overrode it. "I, uh, I gave him a message this afternoon. Was paid by a French toubab. Told him he was supposed to meet you somewhere."

"Where?" It was not a question, but a demand to answer.

So strong was her dominance that he almost blurted it out, but he caught himself in time. He had his share of courage. "I'm just a poor beggar, with no way to feed my family. Look!" He held up two stumps that used to be hands. "I'm a *gana,* no fingers left to work with. Have pity on me for the love of Allah."

Rocky held up a one thousand-franc note. "Where?" she repeated.

"Prices are so high, the taxes are due soon. Do you know that I have to pay the police a hundred francs a day just to be allowed to make a living?"

This time Rocky held five thousand francs. "Tell me now, old leper, or I'll see that your arms and legs and eyes are eaten away, too!"

"The abandoned cigarette factory on the *Route de Rufisque*," he said quickly. He snatched the note and hobbled away as fast as he could go.

By this time Aletha had come down and had seen Rocky give the beggar the money. "What was that all about?" she began.

"No matter. We have to hurry. Do you know where the cigarette factory is?"

"Yes, but..."

"Do you have a car?"

"Yes, it's right down the street, but..."

"Then let's go!" Rocky pulled Aletha with her.

"...but..."

On the way, Rocky told her she thought Demba, and perhaps Lee, too, might be held prisoners there. Actually, she didn't think it likely that Lee was really there, but she knew Aletha's cooperation would be better if the latter thought so.

"There it is," said Aletha finally, pointing to the dark shape across the road. "Shouldn't we have called the police, or Demba's office?"

"No time. And the men would have screwed it up anyway. As it is, we may be too late. Park about fifty meters past it, by that tree there."

They got out of the car and Aletha watched with amazement as Rocky stripped down to her leotard. Silently, Rocky motioned her to follow and they made their way carefully to the side of the building. The night was moonless and Rocky was almost invisible. If Aletha hadn't been holding her hand she would have lost her in seconds.

Just as they came around to the rear of the factory they heard a wrenching cry of pain, followed by a blubbering sound that could have been a man sobbing, and then muffled voices. Rocky led Aletha to a spot some twenty meters opposite the door and whispered in her ear. "I'm going to stand by the door to get them when they come out. You won't be able to see me, so I'll toss a stone for a signal. When you hear it fall start screaming your head off and shake these bushes for all you're worth. Scream as loud as you can, got it?"

"Okay, but..."

"Shhhh!" Rocky went back and stood beside the door. With one hand she picked up a good-sized rock and with the other she drew her knives. She tossed the rock and waited. Nothing. Hadn't Aletha heard it? She was in the act of bending down for another rock when Aletha's piercing scream vibrated through the night. She was nearly caught off guard when the door flew open and two men came running out. She missed her first throw, but the second knife caught the farthest man in the center of the back. The other man turned in time to get her last knife in his throat, and he fell to the ground clutching at it in vain. An instant later she was crouching in the kerosene-lit room.

In a brief second her eyes recorded the scene. Demba suspended from the ceiling with his legs spread and his testicles swollen to enormous size, the vague shape of a man behind him, and the wide-eyed man in front swinging at her with a hose.

To his surprise and dismay she wasn't there when it hit. He was even more dismayed when her foot buried itself in his soft parts, and he gave up all feeling as her elbow crushed his windpipe. She was turning with gun in hand toward the man behind Demba when his voice stopped her cold.

"Enough!" He spoke in French. "A good attempt, but short of victory. Drop your gun and stand up slowly or I will blow your head off." The lantern was on a table right behind Rocky. She could see that it was a Frenchman holding a military .45. Her fingers were just loosening around her pistol when Aletha came to the door.

"Rokhaya, is everything all right?"

The Frenchman snapped off a shot toward the door and in the same moment Rocky threw the lantern at his head. It was a direct hit. The glass shattered against his face, blinding him. He staggered back, cursing, and then plunged clumsily through a door leading to the interior of the factory. The lantern fell on the rubbish-strewn floor and a blaze sprang up.

"Aletha! Cut Demba down and get him out of here!"

"H-how?" She was shaken from the shot that barely missed her.

"Use one of my knives!" Then Rocky went after the Frenchman.

The interior of the factory was completely dark and soundless, except for the faint crackling of the fire. Rocky crept softly along a corridor between some machinery. Her groping hands touched a can. She picked it up and tossed it, hoping the man would fire at the sound. The can fell and clanked a bit, but there was no shot. Too bad, he was smarter than she liked. She would have to draw his fire the hard way. She checked a ten-foot area of the corridor to make certain there were no dangerous obstacles, then climbed up on one of the machines at one end of the safe space. "Toubab!" she cried, and leaped in an arc back down to the corridor. The spot she leapt from exploded in sparks and the boom of the .45 echoed throughout the building. But she had seen the flash of his gun. She headed in that direction as quickly and quietly as she could. An acrid sensation bothered her nostrils. The first wisps of smoke were drifting in from the room where the fire was. She wouldn't have much more time to finish this.

Somewhere in front of her she heard a scraping sound and realized that the Frenchman must be moving, too. She would have to pin down his position again. Her foot struck another can, but this one was filled with something. Gingerly she reached into it and found it was filled with ball bearings. When in doubt, sow confusion, she thought. She grabbed a handful and threw them high and wide. The noise they made as they tumbled and rolled was terrible. She grabbed another handful and ran while the noise was still echoing. He was close by now, she could hear him breathing on the other side of the machine she was next to. Feeling around, she discovered a two-foot steel bar used as a lever for the machine. It came loose without a scrape. Once more she threw the ball bearings and climbed on top of the machine while their din resounded. The light from the fire was reflecting off the galvanized roof and she could see her quarry below her, his gun arm stretched out along the side of the machine. She swung the steel bar down across his wrist and heard it clatter to the floor as he yelped. Rocky jumped down between the man and the gun.

What he saw in front of him was just a woman, and a black woman at that, holding a short rod in front of her with two hands. He had been trained to take on two armed men, if necessary, so although his right hand was numb and blood was dripping into one eye he felt capable of getting rid of her. He feinted, moved to attack, and was suddenly assaulted by a maelstrom of sharp and powerful blows to his ribs, his kidneys, his stomach, his head. He groaned and fell against the machine and Rocky was on him in a second with one end of the rod wedged in a machine crevice and the other held in her hand. The center of the rod was against his throat. The steel bar was again playing the role it was designed for.

"And now, *mon pauvre francais,* why were you torturing that man?"

"Go to hell, *negresse!*"

"Such a strong-willed toubab." Rocky reached one hand down the front of the man's trousers and latched onto a testicle. She dug her fingernails into it and he gagged in agony. "I have strong hands, you see. I can easily turn your balls to jelly." And she gave another squeeze to prove her point.

"Al-al-all right. I was trying to get information on Leland Loring."

"For whom?"

"For... for the French. I am with the *Deuxieme Bureau.* I have contacts who can give you more information than I can. Let me go and I'll take you... Aaargghh!"

"Do not talk so much. I haven't time. Why is Loring so important?"

"We think he is with the CIA, trying to get

something which is necessary to French security. It doesn't involve youououououou!"

"I'll decide that. Would this 'something' be a mask?"

"Then you know? Ah *merde.* Yes, it is a mask which belongs to a secret society, and we know Loring has been in touch with one of the leaders of that society, a man named Baba N'Dow."

"The Lebou sorcerer?"

"Yes, but no one can find him. Loring is our only lead. Look, the fire is getting closer. Please, let me go. Help us find the mask and I'll see that you get all the money you'll ever want."

"That shows how little you know about my tastes. Sorry, *francais,* it's time to say goodbye."

"Don't leave me to burn!"

"No, not that. It would be too cruel. Just this for my poor Demba." She crushed the man's ball in her hand and cut him off in the middle of a scream with a sharp forward snap of the lever. At least he would never feel the fire.

The fire *was* getting close. Rocky took the rod, ran to a window, and used it to pry the boards loose and smash away the remaining shards of glass. Then she jumped out and dashed around to the back. Aletha was sitting about ten feet from the door sobbing, with Demba stretched out before her. She looked up when she heard Rocky and cried out, "Rokhaya! Oh my god, I thought you were in there. I got Demba out, but I couldn't pull him any farther. He's so heavy!"

"That's okay, Aletha. You saved his life. Just a moment." Rocky went and gathered up her knives.

Thanks to the fire she even located the one that missed. Good knives like these were hard to find. "Now, let's get out of here before the police and fire trucks arrive." With a lot of effort the women managed to get Demba's arms over their shoulders and they dragged him to the car. All the way back into town Rocky kept saying, "Ah my Demba, poor Demba. How are we going to make love with you like that? Will we ever be able to make love again?"

They drove straight to Demba's office where Bocar was still working. Fortunately, Demba's agency had a doctor on call for just such emergencies and he was soon being well taken care of in a private clinic. Rocky gave Bocar the barest details of what had happened, saying nothing of her conversation with the Frenchman. She found out from him that they had had no luck in locating Baba N'Dow.

The next day Rocky called Sami and told him everything. He said that as far as he knew Lee didn't have anything to do with the CIA. Aletha had told her the same thing, but she still wasn't sure. Sami spent the rest of the day trying to get in touch with Tamchakett, but to no avail.

The following afternoon Jean-Pierre flew in and gave Sami the message that Lee and the others had moved to a different site. He had some unkind words to say about Lee taking away his girl, however. Sami happily called Rocky and Aletha to tell them that Lee was okay. Demba was still under sedation.

Toward evening, Sami was going over some invoices for imported goods when one of his sons came in and announced a visitor. "There's a *nar* wants to see you," he said, using the Wolof expression for a Mauritanian.

"I'm not interested in silver bracelets, you should know that!"

"He says it's about Loring."

Sami looked up in surprise. "Then show him in."

The Moor entered, looking like any one of a thousand petty merchants in the city with his dirty blue robe and sloppy turban. He sat down in the chair that was offered him, though it was apparent that he would have preferred the floor. Then, in a soft sing-song voice that sounded like he was reciting a memorized speech, the Moor said that he was speaking for the voice of his master, Sheik Abdul El Kerim, leader of all the Regueibat and descendant of the prophet Mohammed, and proceeded to relate the story of the Touareg raid, the killing of Aliberti and the Chinese, the kidnapping of Darla and Salif, and the finding of Loring by his sheik. At that very moment, he continued, Loring and a nephew of the sheik were on a heroic journey into the desert to punish the Touaregs, save their friends, and regain the "Face of God." Their fate was in the hands of Allah the Merciful, the Compassionate. If they lived, they should be in Timbuctu in three weeks. It would be good if they could be met by friends, he ended, but who could foresee the will of Allah?

It sounded so much like a fairy tale the way it was presented, that Sami had to ask, "How do I know this is true?"

"Truth and untruth are not my concern," said the Moor. "I only obey my sheik." And refusing any compensation for a service to his master, he left. That is probably what convinced Sami more than anything.

In a short while, Sami was gathered with Aletha, Rocky and Demba at the latter's bedside. He repeated the Moor's story to them.

"It fits too well," Rocky said. "I'm inclined to believe it."

"Me, too," agreed Aletha. "I never did trust that woman."

"It sounds like the sort of thing Lee would do," sighed Demba. "I think it's true."

Sami scratched the stubble on his chin. "Then someone will have to go and wait for him in Timbuctu and help him, if necessary. I have relatives in Mali and my sons can take care of business here, so I'll set up the welcoming."

Rocky spoke up quickly. "I am definitely going. I have to find out about Darla." She wasn't about to tell them of her interest in the mask.

"I'll have to stay here," said Aletha, "but I can give you the names of the artisans in Timbuctu that Lee deals with. He might try to get in touch with them."

"In three weeks I might be ready to go, too."

A chorus of no's greeted Demba's statement. "You stay here for another full month," insisted Rocky. "I want you ready for me when I get back." That caused everyone to laugh and saved Demba the need for argument.

"Well, I wanted to get into the race and here I am," Sami said before leaving. "I only wish I knew who all the other jockeys were."

9/Sahara

Well, here I am again. After leaving El Kerim's camp Daoud and I traveled on into the night until I almost fell off my camel from fatigue. Then we camped so I could get some much needed sleep and at dawn the next day we continued. My body was still sore, but at least my arm wasn't giving me any pain. I had decided not to fight the fact that I was doing what I was doing, not to make any judgements about whether it was right or wrong, good or bad, stupid or dangerous. A long time ago I discovered that you can't change what already exists. You can only change what it will become. If you try to fight against what already is, it only makes you sick and drains you of whatever energy you have to make it better. So here I was on a camel trip with a broken arm and a young boy chasing a gang of bandits. Not wanting to be there or getting angry about having been forced to do it would not help me to survive it, and I intended to survive. The thing to do was not to resist the fact in front of me, but to reach into it for a way out. And to extract whatever enjoyment from it that I could.

I concentrated on the tasks at hand, moving through them one by one and making them as easy as possible. Checking the loads and harness of the camels (though Daoud did most of that), rationing the food and water, setting up and striking camp, watching the changing terrain of the trail and the shifting shape of the horizon. I concentrated on these present things and on the future. It was probable that we would meet our quarry sometime, so I planned what we would do in different circumstances. I guess you could call it practical daydreaming. I'll tell you one thing, it sure beat worrying.

Daoud turned out to be a pleasant companion. For a desert trek, that is. In Dakar I would rather have Demba or Sami or Aletha, or Dominique, or Suzette, or Annmarie, or... But I wasn't in Dakar. I was in the Sahara riding a camel and Daoud was a good companion.

He never refused or grumbled or criticized my ignorance of the intricacies of camel care. While I can't say he always had a smile on his face, he did once in a while and even laughed occasionally. We swapped insane stories of imaginary adventures we both had had, each trying to top the other and seeing who could rouse a belly laugh. I recited as much as I could remember of "Dangerous Dan McGrew" and "The Midnight Ride of Paul Revere" (try translating *them* into Hassania!) but he far outdid me in that realm. The Moors seem to be natural poets. Perhaps they are inspired by the majestic loneliness of the great desert.

One poem of his went like this:

> *Ana, bouia, ia qaouiou*
> *Fel qeidat jbar tenzahou*
> *Ou ana, cabi, ou ec-cabiou*
> *Ale melleti ie bahou*
> *Berhet el oule cheft el arrad;*
> *Cheft cedar hadi narjaha*
> *Edt ella ouagef ou nkarrar*
> *Ia qaouiou! men nedaha!*
> (My father, O God,
> Found the best there is among women.
> I am still young, and a young man
> Should follow in the footsteps of his father.
> Last evening I saw a woman.
> I saw the breasts of the one I desire.
> I stayed there, erect, repeating:
> O God, what a joy to have her!)

This one put us both in a silent blue funk for a while after he recited it. Our enforced celibacy was bad enough without being reminded of it. By tacit mutual agreement we didn't discuss women again.

There is not much to say about our rambling progress toward Oualata. It took us a week to go three hundred and fifty kilometers. No excitement no danger. Just rolling dunes, and hills, and a lot o:

space. Oualata itself is an ancient village of stone houses with low doorways located on a rocky plateau. We took our rifles apart and stowed them in the saddlebags before entering town. No one paid us any attention. We barely got any glances from the small police contingent. My looks are such that, with a good tan, I could pass easily for a pureblood Berber. I let Daoud do the bargaining for new provisions, however. My accent would have given me away. Daoud loaded us up with dried camel meat, cheese, and a rich date and honey mixture that would stick to our ribs.

We spent the night in Oualata, sharing a hot meal of roast goat with a hospitable merchant, and took off for Charaioun in the morning. In half a day we were there, which was a few scraggly palms surrounding a rock-lined well. The water was raised by means of a rope attached to one end of a long pole made from the trunk of a palm. A pile of rocks was secured to the other end and a stump served as a fulcrum. Just a finger touch on the rocks would draw the opposite tip of the pole some twenty feet into the air and bring up a dripping goatskin full of water. Some Moorish nomads were resting around the well when we got there and while I watered the camels, Daoud found out that one of them had seen a party of riders the size we were looking for leave the area of the well two days before. He had seen them at quite a distance, however, and couldn't supply any details. It had to be our bandits.

From Charaioun we had two choices. The well of El Ragg, or Nefset, each about a hundred kilometers apart. It would mean a loss of two more days if we chose the wrong one, and we already had two days to catch up on. Daoud and I mounted and rode well out of sight of the other nomads. Finally, we came to a halt.

"Now is the time to use your power," he said.

"Daoud, I haven't any power. I don't know which direction to take any more than you do."

"My uncle said that your body would tell you."

"Right now my body is telling me that I should have stayed home. Look, if I choose wrong my friends are dead and the mask is lost."

"And if you choose right, we can save them."

"Yeah, there is that side of it. Oh well, fifty-fifty's the best odds we can get, I suppose." More out of a sense of obligation than faith, I got my camel down on its knees and dismounted. Then I sat down in the sand with my legs crossed, facing east. El Ragg was toward my left and Nefset toward my right. I relaxed and began to breathe in the particular rhythm I had been taught, reciting some words I didn't understand over and over. My eyes were closed and I concentrated my thoughts on the mask. I had never seen it, so I just pictured the canvas bag. In a few moments I felt the familiar lassitude take over my body and soon I was no longer aware of it at all. I was adrift in a world of breath and sound and moving images. My mind focused on an image of the canvas bag that became more and more real, until I could see the detailed texture of the cloth and the threads where it had been sewn together. The bag seemed to be moving oddly, and then the image grew so that I saw it was hanging by a strap on the saddle of a camel being ridden by Maria. The image grew some more and I could see Raoul and the five Touaregs and Salif behind one of them. But I couldn't see Darla. I started to wonder where Darla was when the logical part of me broke through and told me this was only a product of my imagination, and not to get so wrapped up in it. Then I became anxious about my body that I couldn't feel and turned my attention back to it, only to discover that my whole right side was buzzing like it was attached to a vibrator. I snapped back into full awareness and opened my eyes. My throat was dry and I was a little scared, because I had obviously done something and I didn't understand it.

"Daoud," I croaked. "Water."

The boy jumped to loosen a guerba and I drank deeply. It was crazy. I didn't want to trust what I had experienced, and yet I had to. The lives of my friends were dependent on my hallucinations, I thought. What a way to fight a war. Daoud was looking at me expectantly. He was all faith. Whatever decision I made would be the right one. I did my best to hide my uncertainty. "Nefset," I said. And we remounted.

The well was over two hundred kilometers away and we drove ourselves and our camels hard to shorten the distance between us and the troup in front. A day and a half after leaving Charaioun we came across the remains of a camp, no more than some scattered bits of charcoal and several piles of crap on hard ground. There was no way of telling whether it belonged to the people we were chasing, but it gave us hope.

Another half day later the hope was replaced by a terrible certainty. We had come to the top of a rise and Daoud was scanning the horizon. It had always been a wonder to me how the nomads found their way among all that nothingness until I learned that a big key was the shape of the horizon. And like good river pilots who must keep track of changing sand bars, a good desert pilot was expected to stay aware of shifting dunes. Anyway, Daoud was scanning and I was checking the pack camel, a bad-tempered female I called "Lola" because she always did things her own way. What Lola wanted now was to get rid of the bindings and rest awhile. She had bitten through one of the bindings and a saddlebag was coming loose. When I approached she snarled and gurgled as if to warn me not to get any closer. I snarled back and reached out to retie the strap. That's when the bitch clomped down on my arm, just enough to make me drop her reins. Then, with head held high in triumph, she turned away and trotted down into a little wadi, or ravine, that we had passed. I ran after, cussing out her ancestors.

Rounding a bend in the wadi, I came to a sudden, shocking halt. Lola had stopped to graze on a dry bush. What stopped me, though, was a naked body staked out on the sand, about fifteen feet to the right of her. "Oh God!" I burst out, and ran up to it. It was Darla, lying face up and char-broiled to a crisp, lobster red. Blisters had already formed on her breasts and across her hips and her body was covered with ugly welts and scratches. I knelt down beside her. Her eyes remained closed.

Lola held still while I undid a guerba and rushed back to Darla. I dabbed a little water on her lips and then she was straining her head up for more. I gave it to her, making her take it in little sips until she laid her head back. Then I stood and yelled for Daoud as loud as I could. While waiting for him I went back to Lola and took down the small tent we carried. The camel was acting very smug and I couldn't hold it against her. If she hadn't broken away Darla would have died without ever being found.

By the time Daoud arrived I had the tent set up over Darla's body. When he saw her his jaw dropped and his eyes bugged out, whether because of her condition or because he had never seen a nude woman I didn't bother to ask. "Stop staring and get that ointment I've been using," I growled. He shook himself and ran to do it. Minutes later we had covered her skin with the soothing balm, but I knew she must still be in great pain. I took off my burnoose, soaked it in water and gently laid it over her. The evaporation would help to cool her off a little, but we couldn't afford to repeat it more than once.

She seemed to drift off to sleep, so for the next two hours Daoud and I debated what to do. There didn't seem to be any choice. We would have to stay here until Darla was ready to ride, perhaps in two or three days, and then we would head on to Timbuctu. We would lose the mask, but I couldn't see how that could be helped. We certainly couldn't leave Darla here. I couldn't go on alone because I didn't know the route, and I couldn't send Daoud because of the same reason, not to mention the fact that he wouldn't be able to handle Raoul if he met him.

So we had resigned ourselves to failure when I heard Darla cry out my name in a weak voice. I ran over. "Hi, how're you doing now? They must have been pretty rough on you."

"It was almost enough to make a girl give up sex," she rasped. "Let me have some more water." I got it for her and she drank thirstily. When she finished she looked deep into my eyes. Her old sparkle was slowly coming back. "Thanks, Lee. I owe you one."

"No debt, Darla. Lola the camel saved you." And I explained how the balky camel had led me to her.

"You still could have left me. I might've left you, you know."

I knew that, and it hurt in a way. If she had found me in the same situation, she might have untied me, treated my burn and given me water, if she had the time—but she would have gone on with her mission instead of waiting for me to get well. But I'm not made like that. Somewhere in the past I guess my mother programmed me with a different ethic. "Can't help myself," I said. "I get turned on by sunburns."

Darla smiled. "Men are the real romantics in this world." A cloud passed quickly over her features. "Some of them, anyway," she muttered. "How long since you found me?"

"About two hours."

"Then let's go. We can still overtake them if we push hard."

This female never failed to startle me. "What are you talking about? You're in no condition to ride! You've got blisters and..."

"Lance the damn blisters and let's move! There's more at stake here than my comfort. I still don't quite know what this is all about, but that Italian is turning into a madwoman and she has some kind of power that I don't understand. I saw her knock a Touareg clean off his feet with just a touch and now they are all treating her like a sort of goddess. Even her European friend. It's uncanny!"

My first thought was that Darla was still suffering from the effects of the sun. "Look, I admire your spunk, but you've got to rest before you..."

"Lee!" Her eyes were blazing and her voice was intense. "I can tolerate a soft heart, but not a soft brain. I'm telling you that woman is dangerous! She has something she carries with her in a canvas bag. I think it's some kind of electronic device that acts on the nervous system. It seems to block out conscious control over the body. I know, I experienced it!"

The canvas bag? That was supposed to contain the mask. "What do you mean?"

Darla took a deep breath, as if to give her strength for what she was about to say. "The last night that we camped she came over to me carrying that bag and ordered the Touaregs to untie me. I had already given up hope of surviving the trip, so my immediate reaction was to spring on her and break her neck before anyone could stop me. Only... only I couldn't move!" Darla's voice had grown soft. "My muscles just wouldn't obey me. When she told me to get up and walk over to where her friend, Romano, was sitting I almost felt like I was in somebody else's body. She had me take my clothes off and his, and then she had me make love to him in front of all the others. I wasn't numb. I wasn't numb at all. I could feel everything, but it was like I had no will of my own. I did everything it's possible to do to a man.

Naturally, the Touaregs were going out of their heads. When Romano was exhausted she had me run right to them and released her control just as they attacked me. That was rough, believe me!" She paused and closed her eyes for a moment. "Then later, when we reached this spot, she made them stake me out and everybody took another turn." Darla looked at me again. "Lee, what she did to me was just for amusement. I'll kill her for that if I can, but if that machine falls into more ambitious and organized hands we're going to see a totalitarian government like you'd never believe!"

There was no use telling her the bag contained a mask. On the other hand, for all I knew it did contain an electronic device. I had never seen it. Either way, it was turning out to be more important than I thought, and Darla was right. Priority one was to get that bag away from Maria, and out of the hands of anyone else. Including the Lorelei, I added to myself. "Okay," I sighed. "Lay down and I'll lance those blisters."

Twenty minutes later we were all mounted. I had introduced Darla to Daoud, but the language barrier limited their conversation to hand signals and smiles. Darla wore my burnoose and I went without, because we hadn't brought any extra clothing. She was on Lola, who minded less than I had expected, and every movement was obviously painful for her. But she insisted she was up to it so I didn't waste any more sympathy on her. We prodded the camels to a gallop across the sand.

Ever gallop on a camel? Well, either don't, or, if you have a tendency toward sea-sickness, be sure to

182

take Dramamine if you do. Camels don't gallop like horses. They move both legs on one side together and staying aboard is a matter of concentration, skill, and pure luck. I only fell off once when my camel changed its stride and I forgot to compensate. And from that height it's a mean fall. I was lucky that I didn't break my other arm.

After forty hours of constant travel, broken only by very brief rest stops for the sake of the animals, we were approaching Nefset in the noonday heat. The well was located in a shallow hardpan valley, or rather a dip in the terrain. Leaving Darla with the camels a good distance away, Daoud and I crawled up to the edge of the dip with our rifles. About three hundred yards from us there were two tents set up near the wall. Beyond them and to the left we counted eight camels sitting peacefully chewing their cuds. The number of camels was right, if you included a pack animal. Now we had to wait to see who would come out of the tents.

A half hour or so passed. My eyes were tiring from the strain of watching through the heat waves. I lowered my head to rest a moment and Daoud poked me with his foot. On looking out I saw a man leave one of the tents and head for the well. It looked lik a Touareg, but was he one of "ours?" I pulled Daoud down below the rim and told him to move off to my left so we could catch them in a crossfire. But he wasn't to fire until I did.

We waited some more. At last a man came out of the second tent, walked to a point opposite the well, and began to relieve himself. He, too, was dressed like a Touareg, but something didn't seem right.

Suddenly I realized he was still standing. Moslem Touaregs always squat. It had to be Romano!

At that moment he looked in my direction. Whether he saw my turban or not I don't know, but he froze. And I fired.

Romano spun around and fell. I could hear his cry. Then he got up and ran for the cover of the tent. I cursed my broken arm and fired again, but I missed. At about the same time Daoud's rifle sounded off and I saw the man at the well flip over and lie still. At least the boy could shoot. Seconds later the other four Touaregs erupted from the tent, rifles in hand, and started firing back. I shot and killed one who was kneeling, ducked down and ran to a new position. Bullets zipped all around the place I had been. Daoud missed his next shot and they concentrated their fire on him. I don't know what got into him then. Maybe fear, maybe excitement. But he got up and started running toward me. "Get down, you idiot! Get down!" I yelled. No use. I heard the ugly hoomp! of bullets striking flesh. Daoud stumbled and fell with a surprised look on his face. I shot off a couple more quick rounds just to let the bastards know I was still around, and ran over to Daoud. He had been hit twice in the chest and bloody bubbles formed around the holes as he breathed.

He looked at me in wonder. "So this... is what it is like to die," he wheezed. "I shall miss... the dawn... but I look forward to the houris!" He smiled, and died, a young poet fighting for something he didn't even understand.

"Allah give you peace and pleasure," I murmured.

I crawled back up the slope in time to see the remainder of the party mounting their camels. One man was too slow and I picked him off just as his camel was starting to rise. The last two Touaregs were already heading out of the basin and I thought I could see Salif riding with one of them. Romano and Maria—I recognized her white turban—were riding out in a different direction. I shot at Romano, but missed again.

Stopping only to get Daoud's rifle and ammo, I ran back to Darla. "Where's Daoud?" she cried.

"Shut up and catch!" I threw her the rifle and ammunition belt. "Now you'll really have a chance to prove you have guts." I mounted and we rode into the deserted camp, pausing to pick up a full guerba of water and exchange camels. Fortunately, the camels of the first two Touaregs we killed were still hobbled and their saddles had never been removed. It didn't take us more than ten minutes before we were on our way after the mask. Salif, I said to myself, you're on your own. I'm sorry.

Romano and Maria were already out of sight. This was an area of rolling, brush-covered dunes. Their trail was fairly easy to follow, but we only caught sight of them once during the whole rest of that day, and that was at a good distance. When the sun was setting I realized that we would no longer be able to see the trail, but they could keep going and increase their lead. We kept going as long as I could sense anything that faintly resembled a track to follow and then I called a halt.

"We'll stop here for the rest of the night," I told Darla. "They'll probably stop, too, since they'll know we can't follow." That last sentence was really for my own encouragement more than anything else. Darla didn't answer, though. I turned around to look and she was swaying on the saddle. I got both our beasts to kneel and sit, then went over and lifted Darla off. "How're you doing, tigress?"

"Li'l dizzy, 's'all," she answered, and passed out. I had left Lola and the stuff she carried at the well, bringing only our food pack plus the guerba I had picked up. In the rush I hadn't even thought to pick up extra clothing for Darla. She was still nude under my burnoose. I pulled off the sheepskin saddle covers from our mounts and put Darla between them, making her as comfortable as I could. Hanging from my saddle I found a pouch containing tobacco, a Moorish pipe that looked more like a cigarette holder, and, best of all, flint and steel. I gathered up some brush and spent ages making tinder as fine as I could get it, and many more ages getting it lit. Many people remark on the seemingly infinite patience of desert tribesmen. I think it comes from trying to light fires. I was very glad there was no wind this night.

Finally I had a little blaze going that gave off a comfortable warmth. I settled myself against the side of my rumbling camel and relaxed enough to be aware of the setting. It was like we had been transported a thousand years or more into the past. A man, a woman and their resting camels camped around a tiny fire in the vast quietness of the desert under a sky overflowing with stars. The sense of being another person in another time was so strong that I had to pat my passport several times to remember who and when I was. I chewed on some jerky for awhile, smoked a pipeful of powdery tobacco, and fell asleep counting meteors.

It was still dark when I woke, but there was a glow in the east. Darla was already up and had stirred the fire back into life. "Morning," I said. "How are you?"

"Cold and horny. Believe it or not. Do you know this is the first time we've spent a night together without sex?"

"I should think you'd want to give your *toukke* a rest."

"I do, but it doesn't. Maybe I'm a nymphomaniac."

"Could have told you that a long time ago."

She laughed, a sweet, womanly sound that touched off certain nerve centers which would have made it embarrassing to stand up in polite society. Maybe I'm a satyromaniac, I thought. What a combo! But reason prevailed. At least that's what I've been taught to call it.

"C'mon, kid." I got up and stretched. "Time to move on and play another game of Search and Destroy. We can lolligag another day."

"Promise?"

"Promise, you insatiable nymph!" We got things ready and I noticed that one of our camels was female. So we had milk for breakfast. Camel's milk is warm, odiferous, and, um, tastes just like camel's milk. What else can I say?

During the next three days we had no glimpse of Romano or Maria, and to top it off we had lost their trail. Twice in that time I stopped in the middle of the day to sit and meditate on the mask. Once my feelings told me we were headed in the right direction, and the second time the sensation was far to the left of the path we were taking. I hoped Romano knew where he was going. Both times Darla asked me what the hell I was doing. I refused to answer and she muttered something to the effect that I was getting too much sun. But she didn't question the change in route. The wind was blowing steadily now, and because we couldn't build a fire we slept together for warmth. One night the warmth grew beyond just body heat and we made love. I tried to be as gentle as I could so as not to hurt her. Afterward she cried, the first time I had ever felt tears on that pretty face. No, I hadn't caused her pain, she said in answer to my question. Just how stupid was I?

Before noon of the fourth day we rode down the face of a dune and saw mountains in the distance, perhaps twenty or thirty kilometers away. From then on we were on rocky ground and had to pick our way carefully. I remembered my geography well enough to know that we had to be in Mali. Which meant that Timbuctu couldn't be terribly far away. Toward midafternoon we were approaching the foot of the mountains when I saw a brown, bulky heap ahead of us.

"Looks like a dead camel." It was. And still warm. No way to tell why it had died, but it meant that our prey would be slowed down. If they were smart, they would hole up in the rocks and wait to ambush us, supposing they had seen us coming across the rocky plain. The only safe thing was to assume they had.

"We'd better split up here and ride a few hundred yards apart. Less of a target in case they're waiting for us. Can you handle the camel alone?" Up to now I had been holding her reins.

"I have to, so I will. This is your country. What do we do when we reach the rocks?"

"If neither of us has been shot by then we'll look for a trail. When we find it, I'll go first and you follow about fifty yards in back. If they get me you'll have a chance to get away. Hopefully."

"You're being awfully gallant."

"It's a weakness. Probably be the death of me one day. Git!"

We moved apart and headed forward, watchful for any sign of movement in the bare rocks. Closer and closer we came. The tension became almost tangible. The distance between us and the rocks shortened. Every muscle was aquiver. Nerves were on edge ready to respond to the slightest stimulus. My heart was in my mouth. Nothing happened.

I took my heart out of my mouth and called to Darla. "Here's a path in. Stay behind me and don't get too close." I put my heart back in my mouth and we went on. I remember in high school we used to interview students for the school paper and always listed their "pet peeves". One of my pet peeves has always been following an armed murderer up a mountain canyon where the odds are that he'll get me before I'll get him. Something about it I can't get used to.

My camel was making too much noise, the sun was too hot, the air was too still. I was sweating too much, and feeling generally unhappy with my lot when I felt an unmistakeable tingle all down the front of my body. I reined in the camel, his head reared up, and he caught the bullet that was aimed at me. I was out of the saddle and behind some cover while the animal was still falling. A few minutes later Darla crawled up to me with her rifle. She had heard the shot and had dismounted back behind a bend. We just sat there for a while and then I took off my turban and raised the cloth up with a rifle barrel. It barely made it over our rock when it had a hole in it. They knew where we were. And one of them was too good a shot to take chances with.

I looked around. It would be possible to go back the way Darla came without being seen, and once around the bend I could climb up a finger and maybe get above them. However, because of my arm I couldn't do that and carry a rifle, too. Darla was gutsy, but in her shape it would take her half a day to get on top of the finger and then she probably wouldn't have the strength to pull a trigger. What the hell, I'd throw rocks at them. I couldn't think of anything else to do. Neither could Darla, though she called me several sorts of dirty names for wanting to do it. It's nice to know someone cares.

We set up the rifles some ten yards apart and I left her my ammo. She was to move back and forth between them, firing at irregular intervals in the hope that they would think two of us were still there. "Try not to get killed," I told her, "or they'll know for sure that I'm trying to sneak up on them."

"You might worry about me for my own sake. Never mind. I'll take care of things here. Just throw big rocks."

I put my fist under her chin and gave it a little nudge. "You're a brick," I said, and ducked a left hook.

The firing commenced when I was on my way up the slope. There were enough shots to tell me that she was getting return fire, too. I climbed Mt. Everest several times over and found myself looking right down into a little flat area where Romano was stretched out on his stomach with his rifle pointed downhill. I could even see the dark stain on his right shoulder where I had winged him. Maria was sitting back aways well out of the line of fire, holding on to the canvas bag. I wondered briefly where their camel was.

I moved down as quietly as I could till I was close enough to see the sweat on Romano's face. Maria looked like she was asleep. I picked up a handful of rock and waited until Romano had pulled back to reload. Then I flung it with all my might and hit him on his wounded arm. As he howled and rolled over I leaped into the arena with dagger drawn. Romano was up in an instant with his own dagger out.

"You sonofabitch!" he yelled. "I'm going to rip your guts out!" It was the same old loveable Romano. He hadn't changed.

I saved my breath. This fight wouldn't be won by talking. All in all, I guess you could say we were pretty evenly matched. I knew he was right-handed, but that arm was out of commission. My left arm was broken and I was winded from the climb. Still, I wished I had a machine gun.

A quick glance told me Maria hadn't moved, though her eyes were open. From then on I kept my attention on Romano. We circled each other warily like knife fighters are supposed to do and waited for a chance to do each other in. I feinted, he struck out like lightning and missed my neck by half a hair. He struck again, I sidestepped and in a reflex action I whacked him in the kidneys with my left fist. Hooboy, was that a mistake! He stumbled, but I was blinded with pain. I shook my head and barely moved in time to miss another stab. It went on like this till we both could hardly stand up. We each were dripping blood from various pricks and slices.

I had one more trick that I hated to use. I learned it from a Greek sailor who used it to kill a friend of mine in a brawl in Marseilles. The Greek died with my broken beer bottle in his throat, but his trick was good and I never forgot it. I hated to use it because it was going to hurt me almost as much as Romano.

It was the last trick I had, though. Roman was beginning to wear me down and I was afraid he had more stamina. I waited for the right moment, then thrust my left arm at him. He stabbed and I caught his blade right through my forearm, twisted it up, and plunged my dagger under his rib cage. He fell heavily, ripping my arm apart as he did so. I knelt down to cut his throat and heard his last words, "Neat...I'll have to remember that." And then Romano's spirit left us for whatever realm mean bastards like him go to.

I used his turban to wrap my ripped up arm and took my first good look at Maria. She was still lying where I had first seen her, only now she was clutching the bag to her breast. Her face was haggard and her lips were all puffy and cracked. I guessed they had run out of water or hadn't brought any with them in the rush to get away. Maria wasn't beautiful any more.

"Give me the bag, Maria."

She looked shocked. "No, you fool! Don't you understand? This is power! Power that will let me rule the world. I'll establish an empire, no one will be able to resist me. It's all mine, you see? *I can control you!*"

"Maria, you've flipped out. Give me the mask. You need water and medical help. Give me the mask and I'll get you to safety."

"You'll help me anyway because I demand it. Drop that knife and come here."

It was weird. Suddenly I found myself at her side, helping her up. The knife was no longer in my hand. I saw it back where I had dropped it. What brought me back to my senses I don't know. I remember now a ringing in my ears so loud that I couldn't hear her any more. I let her go and jumped back. She must have screamed at me, but I only saw her lips moving. Then she pulled the mask out of the bag. The gold and silver on it sparkled in the sunlight and the ringing in my ears grew louder. She was bringing the mask up to her face and somethjng in me shouted that that was terribly wrong. She shouldn't do it.

"Maria, don't! For God's sake, don't!"

Maybe she didn't hear me, or maybe it didn't make any difference. As soon as she put the mask to her face I saw her body tremble and shake and then become perfectly still. Them mask fell out of her hands and I could see her face. It was blackened and split, like someone had gone over it with a blowtorch. I got sick and threw up my camel jerky.

Somehow I retrieved the mask, put it back in the bag and headed back down the slope. By this time the ringing in my ears had stopped.

I found Darla with a bullet wound in her thigh. It had gone clean through and the bone didn't appear to be broken. We got our lone camel and started on the last leg to Timbuctu. I'll spare you the horror of that journey. Darla was delirious most of the time. I tried to keep the vision of Maria's blackened face out of mind, but it wouldn't go. Anyway, by some miracle of the gods we made it. Some uncounted days later we entered the outskirts of Timbuctu.

And the first people we met were a bunch of American tourists, complete with cameras. "Oh, look, George, look at that couple," a woman cried. "So old Testamentish. See if you can get their picture."

"Right! Hey you!" George came over and waved a camera in my face. "This camera, want take your picture, okay?" All this was done with a loud voice to make me understand better, and broad gestures, including the circled thumb and forefinger and upraised other fingers accompanying the "okay."

I tried to ignore him and veer away, but ol' George was persistent. He put his hand against my chest and said, "No, no! You stay. I take picture. Pay money!" And he flashed a five-hundred franc note worth about two dollars.

That was too much. I gave him a big grin, stuck my upright mid-finger in front of his nose, and said, "Fuck off, George!" Seeing him drop his camera in the mud was the first civilized pleasure I'd had in weeks.

10/Timbuctu

Timbuctu! (or Timbucktoo or Tombouctou or whatever, depending on where you are from). What a name of mystery that used to be. It represented adventure, fabulous wealth, and the furthest anyone could travel. To "go clear to Timbuctu" became such a common phrase in English that most people probably still think it's only an imaginary place. Relatively few know that it is a real town on the Niger River in the West African country of Mali (where?) and now *you* are one of those privileged few. Lucky!

Let me give you a little background on the place, to set the scene, so to speak. The Touaregs founded it in the twelfth century and they still pretty much dominate the place, but it changed hands a lot down through the years. Timbuctu got its reputation in the sixteenth century when a brilliant black named Askia Mohammed established an empire about the size of France and Spain combined and made Timbuctu into a high-powered intellectual and commercial center. Prominent Arab scholars came there to study and word of its great universities and caravan wealth passed through them to Europe where it stimulated itchy feet. Unfortunately, by the time the first Frenchy reached it a couple hundred years later it had been razed to the ground so many times in various wars that he wrote back to his friends *"Tombouctou ne l'est pas"* (trans: Timbuctu isn't all it's cracked up to be). When he found it, it was a dusty, dirty adobe village, and that's what it is today. You can take a packaged tour there now and wander around the sandy streets wondering what the mystery is all about and why you ever came.

And that's just what I was wondering until we came to the marketplace. Then I spied some watermelons in one of the stalls and remembered that one of the reasons was to get away from camel jerky and date paste. After haggling with a Mossi woman I traded my dagger for two melons the size of cantaloupes and brought Darla to a shady spot where we devoured them like the filthy savages we felt ourselves to be.

"Now what?" asked Darla, when the rinds were paper thin. She still wore my burnoose with the hood pulled up to cover her hair. We looked just like a couple of scraggly Moors and no one paid us any attention.

"First thing we have to do is find a friend. You don't have any papers at all..."

"I don't even have any clothes!"

"... and I have a passport with a Mali visa, but it isn't stamped for entry, so we are both illegal aliens. We can't go to a hotel and we can't go to the police and besides, we don't have any money."

"Can't you sell the camel?"

"I thought of that, but I can't do it directly. The camel traders would notice that it's got a Touareg harness and I'd be accused of stealing it. Nope, got to find a friend."

"Do you have anyone in mind?"

"Yeah, but I'll have to go alone to find him. You stay here and hold the reins. If anyone asks questions just grunt and try to make them understand you're waiting for your husband."

"How long will you be gone?"

"An hour, maybe two at the most. If I can't find him in that time I'll come back anyway."

"Lee," she hesitated and bit her lip. "Couldn't you, uh, couldn't you use the mask to get some help? The way Maria did?"

I thought of Maria's face again. I hadn't told Darla exactly what had happened. "No way, kid. I don't think it works for me, anyway."

"Then what are we going to do with it? You haven't let it out of your hands since you got it from her. That's really why you came after us, isn't it? To get the mask."

"Not the only reason. But the mask belongs to someone and I promised to get it back. Now, stay here, shut up, and don't think so much. See you soon." I picked up the bag with the mask and walked away.

Naturally I had done a lot of thinking about the mask since leaving the remains of Maria and Romano, including how Maria used it to exert her will over Darla and the others. It was, just as naturally, a tempting thought. There was certainly a feel about the mask that I couldn't explain, like it was charged with a palpable electricity or magnetism. Darla and I hadn't talked about it, but I noticed that we were both healthier than we should have been. My arm no longer bothered me. In fact, it felt as good as new. And Darla's leg wound was completely healed, with just a little scar where the bullet had gone through. Was it the desert air or the mask? It wasn't the air that killed Maria. What could have done that? Not magnetism, but electricity could have. But how could a wood and metal mask hold enough electricity to do that? I had checked the mask carefully. It was only wood inlaid and overlaid with what looked like gold and silver. I knew a little about electronics and there was no way a simple combination like that could do what it did to Maria, or to cause someone to do something against their will. Even electricity couldn't do that. It takes energy to burn someone, so we were obviously dealing with a form of energy. But what? I never did and still don't believe in magic, in the sense of being able to cause things to happen outside of physical laws. However, I had to admit there were probably a lot of physical laws no one had discovered yet.

This bright inward chatter brought me to a section of town that was mostly occupied by artisans. It didn't look any different from the rest of town. Mud brick buildings with pointed moorish doorways, half-naked chilluns dashing around, and the smell of dung and urine. But it was where the artisans lived. And I knew one of them. Ousmane Sidi, a Fulani who made ebony doodads for the tourists. The Malien government was encouraging tourism to make a lot of bucks and Sidi was selling them genyoowine ebony dolls and letter openers from Timbuctu. Of course, the fact that ebony didn't grow anywhere near the place and no one in the town had ever seen those kind of dolls before Sidi arrived bothered no one at all, least of all the tourists.

I inquired after Sidi and kept being sent from one building to another until I found his own adobe abode and one of his sons told me he was at the hotel selling his wares. So I headed back the way I came, thinking about the hotel and a hot bath and clean sheets when I rounded a corner and saw her standing up and talking to a smartly-dressed black woman. Coming closer, I saw that it was Rokhaya and was about to break into a happy run when I also saw Darla go back and sit down where I had left her and Rokhaya walk away.

Now, friends and neighbors, that just didn't look right. Both of them should have waited there for me, or even if both had abandoned me it would have been understandable. But I didn't like this. I sat in the shadow of a building where Darla wouldn't be likely to look and waited, just in case Rocky was

199

only going to buy some food or something. After what I considered a reasonable time I took off like a bat for the hotel. Between Rocky's walking and my running I arrived in time to watch her move up the front steps and around to a side terrace. Keeping well away and ready to turn aside if she looked in my direction, I went around the side of the hotel to where I could get a full view of the terrace. Rocky walked right up to a table with a Cinzano umbrella and sat down across from Sami.

Believe me, it took some discipline to keep from running up and grabbing my ol' buddy, especially when I noticed he was drinking a cool-looking bottle of Heineken's, but I did it. Years of near-fatal mistakes had taught me a fair degree of caution. I didn't know what Rocky and Sami were talking about, but I didn't see him jumping up and down so I felt justified in guessing that she wasn't telling him about finding Darla. Unless, of course, Sami was in cahoots with her against me. Wow. It's hell to be paranoid about your friends, yet it does keep you alive sometimes.

I squatted in the shade of an acacia tree and watched them with occasional glances. They looked like they were talking about the weather. Finally, Rocky got up and went into the hotel. Sami stayed where he was and ordered another beer. I did some hard thinking about what to do. At last I heaved a big sigh and decided. Sometimes you can keep alive by trusting your friends.

I looked around and gathered up some balls of goat dung. Without moving from my position I tossed a dung ball toward Sami. It hit him on the leg and he looked up to see me staring at him. He frowned and went back to drinking his beer. I threw another and it landed on his table and rolled across. He got angry this time and yelled at me to knock it off. He didn't recognize me and I didn't blame him. My mother wouldn't have, and if she did she would have refused to acknowledge that I was hers. So I threw three more balls in rapid succession. One hit him on the head, one almost fell in his glass, and the third went wide. Two out of three isn't bad, but I would need more practice before I could enter the international dung throwing olympics.

That did it. Sami got up very red in the face and came stomping over to me. I sat there with my eyes on the ground while he threatened me with bodily harm and called me more vile names than I knew he knew he knew. Then I looked up and said, "Pig turd, Sami. You forgot to call me a pig turd."

He fell like a rock. Straight down with his bottom thumping the sand. "Joseph, Mary, Jesus! It's you! My God, we were afraid you were dead." Tears welled up in his eyes. Hey, hey, this was a friend.

I could see he was about to give me a bear hug. "Hold it, Sami. Keep it cool. I'd rather not be noticed just yet. I'm damned happy to see you, but in case Rocky's looking let's pretend I'm just an uncouth desert rat."

"You are an uncouth desert rat," he said, holding himself back with an effort. "What does it matter if she sees you? We're both looking for you!"

"Right, but maybe not for the same reasons." I told him very briefly about seeing her and Darla and how I felt about it. Then, "Let's cut this short. It won't look natural for you to be here too long. Do you have any friends in town? Right now I need money, food, clothes, soap and water and a place to stay, for me and Darla. But first I need a safe to stash something in."

Sami took out a notepad and scribbled in it. "Man's name is Paul Nazzarin, general store two blocks from the big mosque. Show him this and he'll do whatever you ask." Sami was good at getting right down to essentials.

I pocketed the note. "I'll go there first, then I'll get Darla. Later I'll send a messenger to tell you I'm in town and you can act suitably surprised and pleased. It's okay if Rocky knows by then where I am." Out of the corner of my eye I spotted her coming back out of the hotel. "Hit me Sami, now!"

Quicker than I expected he stood up and walloped me across the side of the head. I rolled, got to my feet and ran. "Pig turd!" he shouted after me. I laughed in spite of the headache.

Nazzarin was more than accomodating. He had a safe big enough for the mask and gave his word not to let anyone know I had stored something there. I left his store with two hundred dollars worth of francs in my pocket and a cold beer in my hand. A couple of his servants were already preparing the baths.

Darla hadn't moved and looked properly hopeful when I showed up. "Any luck?"

"Lots of it. I sold the camel and there's soap and water waiting. Here, have a half a beer."

"Mmm, good! Let's go. I can't wait for that bath. Who's your friend?"

"A Lebanese shopowner. Sold him the camel for enough to buy us clothes and food and a place to stay Then we'll see what we can do about our documents."

For a few moments we walked in silence and then she asked, "What did you do with the mask?"

"I returned it to the other friend I told you about, the one I promised to get it for."

"Lee, that mask is dangerous. You know what the device that's in it can do. How do you know how your friend plans to use it?" Though Darla now knew the bag contained a mask, she still believed its effects were caused electronically. How I wished they were.

"Don't worry, the person I gave it to knows how to take care of it."

"What is he, some kind of saint?"

I thought about that. The person I had given it to was myself. I recalled the old novels by Leslie Charteris and said, "Some kind of."

"Sometimes you are too trusting."

"I think you're right about that." I kept my eyes straight ahead and my expression blank, but out of my side vision I noticed that she threw me a quick, sharp glance. Sometimes I also have too much mouth.

When we reached the store I introduced Darla to Nazzarin and he had a servant girl lead her to the bath. I told her my bath was somewhere else and that I'd meet her in an hour. Then I returned to the hotel.

All this walking back and forth was wearing me out when what I really wanted was to soak in a tub with a bottle of cognac and a dozen damsels to help me forget the rest of the world. But that would have to come later. First I had to find Ousmane. As I approached the hotel I kept a close watch for any sign of Rocky. My feeling was strong now that whatever she and Darla were planning had to do with the mask. I suspected that Lorelei HQ had found out about it and given them a new assignment. Darla was probably supposed to stick with me until she found out what I was going to do with it. That would have been harder if we had been reunited with Rocky and Sami right away. At least, that's how my thinking went.

Ousmane was sitting by a rack of junk art objects outside the entrance to the hotel, engaged in an avid bargaining session with a pretty young tourist who had an English look about her. I squatted some distance away and waited. To pass the time I began mentally undressing her, imagining what it would be like to snuggle up to that trim-looking body and run my fingers through her long, blondish hair. Suddenly she stood up straight and looked directly at me, bringing her hand to her throat in the gesture that girls make when they feel threatened. It was almost as if she had felt my thoughts. I lowered my eyes and when I looked back up she was hurrying into the hotel and Ousmane was yelling after her. Obviously she had left before the sale was completed.

I walked up to the entrance and sat next to Ousmane. "Ousmane Sidi," I said, "if you recognize me don't make a production out of it."

He turned to me irritably. "Get lost. I have no need of... Leland Loring?" His eyes grew big. "But what are you doing all filthy and dressed like a *nar*?"

"Playing games. Look, I want you to do a big job for me. Ten thousand francs down and ninety thou more when you finish."

"Do you want someone killed or kidnapped, or do you want to make love to the governor's wife?"

"Nothing that easy," I grinned, and described exactly what I wanted him to do. While we talked various groups of tourists walked in and out of the hotel. I particularly noticed a group of Russians—three men and a woman—and half a dozen Chinese. Tourists, technicians, or agents after the mask? Even though there shouldn't have been any way they could know about me being alive I felt uneasy.

When Ousmane and I had finished with the details of the project he said, "It will take me a week, at least."

"You have until tomorrow night or the deal's off."

"Crazy man! I'll need lots of help!"

"Add it to the bill, only be reasonable. I'll be at your place at eight tomorrow night to pick it up."

"You're not being reasonable," he muttered, "so I see no reason why I should be. Why are you Americans always in such a rush?"

"We have ants in our pants. See you, Sidi." I paid him the ten thousand and went back to Nazzarin's with twenty minutes to spare on my hour. That good fellow led me to his son's house around the corner and I plopped into a hot, sudsy bath. It was the second most sensuous thing I had ever experienced.

While I was putting on the African suit that was laid out for me Nazzarin knocked on the door. "May I come in?"

"Sure." I let him in. "What's up?"

He looked nervous. "Mr. Loring, I'm afraid I have done something wrong."

"What do you mean?"

"Well, after you left before the young lady you brought here came back out and asked me what you had done with the package. She was so casual, and she was with you, so I told her it was in the safe. Later I thought maybe I shouldn't have done that."

"You're right, but I guess I can live with it. Now that you are here, let's call this my official notification that Sami is in town. Will you please send him a message? We'll need a place to meet. I'd rather not go to the hotel just yet."

"I'd be honored if you'd have dinner with me."

"Thanks, that would be perfect. And by the way, I'd appreciate it if you don't speak to that girl any more than you have to, and warn your family and staff about her, too. She's part friend and part enemy."

He smiled with a nice mixture of contriteness and understanding. "Yes, Mr. Loring. Do you want to do anything about the package?"

"Later. Let's go back to the store now."

Darla was sitting behind a counter, dressed in an ankle-length boubou that she had arranged to look like a sarong with a sort of homemade halter top. Her hair was damp and pulled back and I suddenly wanted to take her to bed. Instead, I ran up and took her hands and said with boyish enthusiasm, "Hey, Darla, I just heard that Sami and Rokhaya are in town! They're going to meet us here for dinner!"

"Oh, how wonderful! My God, what luck!"

Surprise, happiness, relief and even tears in her eyes. Consummate actress.

When Rocky and Sami arrived we all got a chance to do some more acting. We hugged and kissed and shouted and danced and finally got down to eating dinner. During the meal Darla and I told them about our adventures in the desert, though by tacit agreement neither of us mentioned the mask. Then Sami and Rocky told us what had happened in Dakar. Demba was coming along fine, but he was on crutches because walking was still too painful. Sami mentioned that no one had been able to locate Baba N'Dow, and with all eyes on me I just said that it wasn't important. He was only a friend who helped me out.

"How many Lebou sorcerers do you have for friends?" asked Rocky.

Laughing, I said that he was a good source of fetishes for the stateside markets. No more questions were asked.

Over champagne and dessert—Nazzarin was a very good host—we got on the subject of legalities. I handed Sami my passport and he promised to get the visa stamped the next day. Rocky had a fresh one all ready for Darla, part of their emergency rations, I think. It's amazing what you can do when you know the right people. And when you have enough money behind you.

When brandy was served I asked Nazzarin to leave and we got down to the real issue at hand.

"Sami, I heard there were some Russkies and Chicoms in town. Do you know what they're doing?"

"The Russians are supposed to be technical advisors on river transportation, but all they do is wander around the streets and sit in the hotel. The Chinese are part of a cultural exchange mission. I've seen them talking with local officials."

"After what happened to me in Dakar and Aoudaghost I'm inclinded to be suspicious."

"The Moor that told me you'd be here said something about the 'Face of God.' Is that what this is all about? What is it?"

"It's an object I have that has to get back to Dakar. Apparently a lot of people want it and the problem is how to get it there without losing it along the way."

"You said," began Darla.

"It's okay, sweetheart, I know you know where it is. What I don't know is where you and Rocky stand on this."

"We're free agents," answered Rocky. "I called Home and was told to use our own discretion. If you want us to help you get whatever it is you have to Dakar, we'll be gald to do it at standard rates."

I knew that their "standard rates" were a thousand dollars a day plus expenses for guaranteed service with exceptions for Acts of God and unforeseeable circumstances. I couldn't remember whether dental and hospital insurance were included in that, though. Neither did I trust them. If they were after the mask themselves any deal I made would be invalid.

"Okay, it's a deal. If the schedules haven't changed the next plane for Bamako leaves day after tomorrow, right, Sami?"

"That's right."

"Then get us tickets with connections for Dakar. How are chances for getting some hotel rooms for tonight, adjoining if possible."

"Can do. A bunch of tourists left this afternoon for Mopti, so there's space."

"Fine. As long as I'm here I might as well pick up some art for my clients, so I'll want some extra cash, too. I'll pay you back and pay you girls off when we reach Dakar."

"No problem, Lee."

"Then let's thank our host and move to the hotel." Earlier, I had given Nazzarin a list of things I needed from his store, including a suitcase, and they were ready for me when we came out of the living quarters in back. He opened the safe for me, I stuffed the sack with the mask in the suitcase, and after thanking him for everything and telling him he could keep the camel we were on our way.

Oh man, did I sleep that night. The hotel would never make Michelin's list, but as far as I was concerned it was first class luxury. For all I knew the mattress was packed with straw, but after weeks of sand and rocks it felt like down. I slept an untroubled sleep straight through for eleven hours.

By the time I got washed and dressed and into the hotel restaurant Sami and Rocky were sitting down to lunch. Darla was still in bed. I was carrying the mask in a tan vinyl traveling bag with a shoulder strap. "Howdy-do," I said to my friends as I joined them at the table. "I'm keeping this with me, so keep your eyes on, Rocky."

"You've never been in better hands."

On the other side of the dining room two of the Russian men I had seen earlier. Once during the meal I caught them looking hard at me and they quickly turned away. Was there skullduggery afoot?

Darla joined us after another hour—meals are very leisurely affairs in francophone countries—and when everyone was through I gave the orders for the day. "I'm going around town to pick up some more trinkets. Darla will walk with me. Rocky, you wait to see if anyone follows and then come along behind. Sami, stay here and pick up any interesting tidbits of gossip at the bar. Okay? Then off we go!"

We spent the afternoon visiting the tourist bureau and various little silversmiths picking up daggers and bracelets and pendants and ostrich eggs and whatnot, and I gradually noticed that the two Russians who were following us were decreasing the distance. Rocky was somewhere behind them, but they were getting to be an irritation. On one stretch of street I saw a policeman leaning against a building and a group of little boys off to one side and I got an idea.

I went up to the boys, who looked to be around nine or ten. "Anybody here speak French?"

"I do!" said one big brown-eyed kid proudly.

"How would you like to play a trick on some friends of mine?"

"How much?" There are some parts of the world where children are initiated early into the commercial way of life.

"Five hundred francs now and the same later if you do it good. I'll be on the terrace of the hotel at nine tonight and you can pick it up."

"A thousand now and a thousand later." This kid was going to be the Rockefeller of Mali.

"Five hundred now and a thousand later, or you can go back to playing alley-oop." We shook hands. I asked him if he could see those two men behind us and he said yes, so I told him what I wanted him and his friends to do.

Darla and I walked up to the policeman and I asked him how to get to the mosque. Suddenly there were shouts and chatter behind us. A group of kids clustered around the Russians, pulling on their arms and legs and begging for money. They were so surprised they could hardly move. The cop didn't pay any attention to them. I thanked him for the directions and said to Darla, "Let's run so we don't miss the sunset." As soon as we took off the Russians broke out of the circle of children, bowling a couple of them over. The kids screamed like they'd had their arms and legs pulled off. I glanced back and saw the cop bring his gun out of his holster and stop the two men from coming after us. I learned later that they had been taken to the police station followed by an angry mob. I don't mind paying well for good work.

It was nearly eight when Darla asked, "Didn't you do enough walking in the desert? I'm about to drop."

"One more stop. Then we'll call it quits. I don't get to come here very often and the stuff is unique." We arrived at Sidi's and I told her to wait outside while I bargained for some more items. She'd watched the same process all afternoon, so she didn't mind.

Ousmane was sitting inside, looking unhappy. "I was afraid you'd be on time. Don't you know that's not polite?"

"I'll apologize some other time. Is my order ready?"

"It's ready," he sighed. "But I'll never do anything like that again for you, no matter how much you pay. Come and look."

"Not bad, not bad at all. Wrap them up and throw in some more of your best items. I'll need someone to carry it all back to the hotel for me. How much do I owe you?"

"Two hundred thousand."

"Ah *merde,* Ousmane. I don't have time to play 'Screw The Sucker.' I promised you ninety for the one job and I'll throw in another thirty for your extra help and the junk I just bought. For once let's just have a straight payment instead of all the bickering, all right?" Half hour later I had him down to a hundred and fifty thou. At two-hundred fifty francs to the dollar that meant I had saved a couple hundred bucks. We were both pleased.

Darla rolled her eyes when she saw the bundle being carried out by one of Ousmane's apprentices. That was exactly the response I had hoped for.

On the way back to the hotel I was silent, thinking about the last words Sidi said to me. "Leland, you seem very strange this time. I don't mean the way you were dressed and the crazy order you placed. It is something else. Like you have the *baraka* on you."

Baraka is an Arab word meaning "spiritual power." Even Ousmane had felt the effects of the mask. I turned my attention to the bag slung over my arm and felt the by now familiar tingle. Since the affair with Maria I hadn't really thought much about the power of the mask, just the necessity of protecting it. But now the idea of its power was tickling my mind. So far I had heard El Kerim talk about it, I had heard Darla describe what had happened to her, and I had seen what it did to Maria. Other than that all I knew about it was the sensation I felt from it. Did it really have any power? And if it did, what would it feel like to direct it?

At the hotel we put all my purchases of the day in my room and went down to the terrace for dinner with Rocky and Sami. The boy I hired to trick the Russians was there and I paid him off. The other two Russians, a man and a woman, were having dinner, too, and I got some nasty looks from them.

I guess I was really lost in my thoughts while we ate, because Darla startled me with, "Lee, are you all right?"

"Huh? What?"

"You've been sitting there for almost two minutes with a forkful of meat an inch from your mouth. Please, either eat it or put it down. The suspense is killing me."

"Oh, sure. Sorry." I ate it. It was cold.

"Did you hear what I said about the tickets?" That was Sami.

"Uh, no, I didn't. My mind is somewhere else. What about them?"

"We got'em. Plane leaves at ten a.m. tomorrow. There'll be an hour layover in Bamako and then we take an Ilyushin to Dakar."

"A Russian plane? That doesn't sound too wise."

"Best we can do unless we want to wait another day. I don't think they'll try anything on a commercial flight."

"Maybe not," I said, unconvinced. I dropped back into a reverie. How did I know this whole thing wasn't a hoax? I mean, sure, it gave off energy, but that by itself didn't have anything to do with controlling minds. I'd been carrying it for about a week and I didn't feel like I was controlling anybody. Of course, I hadn't really tried. Maybe that was the trick. If I was going to get the mask safely back to Senegal I might have to use it to keep from getting killed. So I'd better find out how to use it first. And all the while these thoughts were swimming around another thought kept trying to push its way forward: Who do you think you're kidding? That one made me feel uncomfortable, so I locked it away and looked around for someone to experiment on. I decided the best test would be with a stranger. One of the Russians? The waiter? A tourist?

Two tables away from us a family was just finishing dinner. An older man and woman got up, leaving a young girl there who opened a book to read. I heard her say she would be along in a little while. It was the same doll I had seen bargaining with Ousmane. She would help me test the mask. As soon as her parents were out of the room I excused myself and went over to her table. At worst I figured I could only get a slapped face. I bent down to her ear and said, "Come to my room, number 211, at midnight." I was holding onto the mask through the vinyl bag.

Her face got beet red and she didn't look up from

the book, but her lips moved. "I'll be there," she whispered.

On the way back to my table I couldn't help wondering whether it was the mask or my innate charm that had made her agree so readily.

"What was that all about?" inquired Darla. "Do you know her?"

"No, I just invited her over for a drink and she told me to beat it."

Darla eyed the girl carefully. "In the States we would call that jailbait."

"I don't think she's that young. Besides, it doesn't matter. Let's get down to business."

"It's about time," said Rocky. "What's the plan of action?"

For the next hour I outlined the exact steps I had in mind for getting the mask back to Dakar and what to do with it then. I didn't intend to follow any of it, but it kept everybody happy. My own plans were quite different.

When we were through we each took off for our separate rooms. Darla wanted to spend the night with me "to help guard the mask" but I succeeded in convincing her that sleep was more important than sex for this night. I sat on my bed and waited for midnight. As soon as I heard the soft knock on my door I realized my heart was beating and my palms were sweating like a kid about to have his first piece. I opened up and she was there, wearing the same sleeveless dress as at dinner. She must have just gone to her room and waited. She was pretty, but she looked awfully young, and very scared.

"Come in and sit down." I gestured to the bed and

she went directly to it. "What's your name?" She spoke too low for me to hear. "Sorry, I didn't hear you. What is it?"

"Kathryn. Kathryn Blythe." Her hand went to her throat in that familiar gesture and she kept her eyes on the floor.

"How old are you, Kathryn?"

"Eighteen. Last Thursday."

Just past jailbait, I thought, relieved. "Kathryn, you're English, aren't you?" She nodded. "Why did you come here?"

She looked up at me, startled. "I ... I don't really know. It's not the kind of thing I've ever done before. I shouldn't be here at all, but you are quite attractive and I suppose I couldn't help myself. I really should be going back." She didn't move.

I had to find out one more thing. "Tell me, Kathryn. Have you ever made love to a man?"

"Once, last summer on a skiing trip. There was this boy from Eton..."

"Okay, you don't have to tell me any more." It was time to test. I felt myself trembling. Hard to believe about an old roue like me, isn't it? It's one thing to make love to a willing woman, however, and quite another to make love to one who has to *obey* you. The sense of power can be both exhilarating and frightening, if you know what I mean. If you don't know what I mean, then just try to imagine it.

"Kathryn, take your clothes off."

She didn't do any such thing. She only sat there and blushed like mad. What the hell? The mask didn't work? I said it again. "Take your clothes off."

"I can't. It isn't right. I can't simply undress in

front of a stranger. Please, I can't do that!" Her fingers gripped the hem of her dress, but they didn't move.

I thought for a minute. This was hardly control. Either the mask didn't work like I thought it did or I was doing something wrong (technically, not morally. I scrupulously kept the moral question out of my thoughts). So I tried another tack. "I'm going to turn around, and when I do I want you to take off your shoes and stockings so you'll be more comfortable, all right?"

"All right." I turned and waited. There were some rustling sounds and when I turned again she was barefoot, her shoes and stockings in a neat little pile on the floor. Now I was getting a better idea of what the mask did. I went a little further.

"Okay, Kathryn, it's all right for you to get undressed if you are alone, isn't it?"

"Of course."

"Then I want you to pretend you are alone and that you're getting ready for bed. Now you can get undressed."

Without any hesitation she unzipped her dress and pulled it over her head, dropping it on the floor. Then she took off her bra and was pulling her pants down over her hips when I stopped her. "Hold it, Kathryn. Close your eyes. You are going to have a dream, a beautiful dream in which you meet a lover who gives you all the erotic pleasures you've ever hoped to have. And you give yourself to him fully and freely, with no reservations, because it's only a dream and you can do whatever you like. When you open your eyes it will be in the dream and you will see me as your dream lover. Now, open your eyes." She opened them wide and stepped toward me. Even in the half-light I could see what shined within them. It was lust.

Three hours later I knew the secret of the mask. After several rounds of things she couldn't possibly have known about, like the Muskrat Ramble and the Teleological Twirl, I wearily called a halt and had her get dressed. At the door, I told her, "When you get back in bed you will go to sleep instantly and when you awake again you will remember everything as a beautiful dream, nothing more. Do you understand?"

"I understand." And she kissed me like few eighteen-year-olds know how.

Lest you are wondering, by the way, about any future effects our love-making might have had, I had decided three years before that the world would be better off without my adding to the population problem, so I had seen a doctor who had fixed me up fine. You can't say I don't have *any* sense of ethics.

Alone, I reflected on the mask. It didn't give absolute control over someone else's mind, but it did seem to intensify the power of suggestion along the lines that people thought in anyway. That could be dangerous enough in the wrong hands because there were a lot of ugly thoughts floating around. Somebody had to control the mask, someone who could be trusted to make sure it would only be used for people's benefit. It certainly had to be kept out of the hands of any government. And how did I know that N'Dow and his secret society wouldn't use it for selfish ends? The only one I could really trust was myself (something inside me laughed at that, but I squashed it). I didn't know *how* the mask worked, but then I didn't know how an automobile engine worked, either, yet I could drive one. Yes, I would be master of the mask and carefully guide the world to a new era of peace and prosperity. I might have to establish a new nation first, and through the use of radio I could reach the rest of the world and lead everyone to...

Without paying attention, I had drawn the mask out of the bag and was raising it to my face. In my mind's eye I think I was seeing myself standing before a vast assembly of people, wearing the mask and having all of them acknowledge my power and righteousness. It was heady stuff. But as I brought the mask to eye level I was hit with the same ringing in my head that had protected me from Maria, only this time it was so fierce that I honestly thought my skull was splitting apart. I barely remember dropping the mask and then world went black and swirly.

It was the smell of vomit that woke me up. At least that was the first sense I became aware of. I was lying across the bed. The sheets were drenched in sweat turned cold and I was shivering. I had thrown up all over my chest. My mouth tasted like yecchh and I didn't feel very much like the master of the world. I checked my watch. It was five o'clock.

In the shower I remembered a dream. I seldom pay much attention to them, but this one was clear, logical and unequivocal. I've never had one that impressed me as much. And now I knew exactly what I had to do. On the way out of the bathroom I looked at myself in the mirror. "Well, idiot, you just about botched that one up good, didn't you?" And my image answered, "Yeah, stoop, you're no better than any of 'em."

The mask was on the floor where I had dropped it. I put it in the bag, got dressed, picked up some other things, and ran all the way to Nazzarin's. There I woke him out of a pleasant sleep and got him to open the safe for me. I was back at the hotel by six-thirty.

It was seven before anyone joined me on the terrace. Rocky was the first one to come out.

"Well, I see you've still got the treasure."

"Natch." I gripped the vinyl bag tighter. "The difficult part will be getting home safe."

"Where do you expect the most trouble?"

"Right after we leave the airport in Dakar. There might be some problems in Bamako, but I think the serious stuff will come later."

"You wouldn't think people could get so excited over a piece of wood."

"People will do the damdest things. In Italy they used to fight wars over scraps of hair and bone. And pieces of cloth with marks on them. They fight wars over them, too."

"But it isn't the objects people are fighting over. It's what they stand for."

"Right. So it isn't this piece of wood I'm carrying that gets people so shook up. It's the power it represents."

"What do you think about power, Lee?"

That was a cute question in the light of what I had recently gone through. "It depends on how you define it," I said carefully. "If you mean the ability to act, then I can't knock it. There isn't enough of that kind of power around. But if you mean control over others, then I tend to go along with Lord Acton."

"You mean, 'power corrupts...'"

"And absolute power corrupts absolutely. Personally, I don't really think people can control others, but the attempt to do so can get kind of messy."

"But people can be coerced and influenced."

"Oh hell, yes. That's the real danger of Acton's kind of power. Say Rocky, what's with the philosophical discourse?" She was beginning to sound like she knew what I had gone through.

"Just passing time, Lee. Oh look, here comes Sami and Darla. I'll get a waiter."

The rest of the morning was spent in a lazy way until flight time. The airport had been nicely constructed to look like a Moorish palace and tourists were snapping pictures all over the place. My little English girl was there, but she paid no more attention to me than if we had never met. I wondered if her dream lover had a different face.

Finally it was departure time. We were riding first class—it's the only way to fly if you have money to throw away—so we boarded first. Rocky and Sami were on one side of the aisle and Darla and I were on the other. I watched out the window till I saw the last passenger heading for the boarding ramp. Then I got a pained expression on my face and clutched my abdomen.

"Oh, oh. I think this morning's coffee is catching up with me. I've got to go back to the head." I took the vinyl bag off my shoulder. "Here, Darla, hold this. And for God's sake be careful with it!"

Midst their surprise I hurried through the first class curtain and back down the aisle. Luckily the plane wasn't too crowded. I only had to knock one old lady out of the way and into the arms of a dumbfounded missionary. The steward was just pulling the hatch closed. I stopped him and shouted, frantically, "Sorry, I just remembered I left my family at the hotel!" The ramp had already been pulled away, so I had to jump. The officials at the gate were upset, but I explained about my family and they let me go with angry remarks about stupid Americans.

I waved goodbye as the plane took off. Then I went to Nazzarin's to pick up my gear and the tickets I had asked him to buy for me. In another couple of hours I would be steaming downriver on the Niger Queen.

11/Bamako and Beyond

There is nothing quite like tooling along on a quiet river, sipping on a gin and tonic in the middle of Africa. Hey, you know I've been here for years and every once in a while I still get a little of the ol' excitement about being where I am. Part of it must be the reliving of old movies I saw as a kid. I've swum in secluded forest pools with baboons screaming on top of vine-covered cliffs just like Tarzan; I've canoed down crocodile-infested streams and stumbled across hidden idols like Jungle Jim; I've ridden boats like the African Queen, watched rhino charges like Frank Buck, and drunk whiskey in portside dives with ancient ceiling fans like Peter Lorre and Sydney Greenstreet. Funny thing is, most of those movies are around thirty years old and I can do the same things today. Africa has gone through a lot of changes... and yet it hasn't. I ran across one tribe in northern Dahomey that wasn't even aware there had ever been any colonialism, much less that the country they lived in was now independent. On the other hand, one of the most famous and picturesque symbols of Africa has all but disappeared: the cork sun helmet. Probably the most practical head-protection devices ever invented, it vanished overnight when independence came because it had also become a symbol of colonialism. I've never been able to find out whether or not its elimination was written into the independence agreements. At any rate, the French replaced it with the canvas wide-brim hats which button up jauntily on one side that they used in Vietnam.

That's what I was wearing now, tipped low over my forehead as I sat on the top deck of the Niger Queen with my chair leaned back and my feet on the rail. Peace and contentment. The boat was chugging along steadily and most of the passengers were sprawled out on the lower decks to escape from the heat and, wherever possible, the sun. Two white cranes were gliding along the shore, their widespread wingtips seeming to brush the surface of the water. All was right with the world.

Except that the same two Russians who had followed me in Timbuctu had boarded in Mopti, and had taken the cabin across from mine. The captain told me they were technicians who were supposed to evaluate the river transportation system with a view toward modernization. He also told me that if they were river experts he was an astronaut. A friendly man, he had lent me his binoculars (for a very modest rental fee) and with them I spotted a motor launch following us at a steady distance. I patted the travel bag that hung at my side. This was the last night before reaching Bamako, and the night they would try to get the mask, if they were going to try.

I don't know what time it was when the slight scraping of the chair I had placed in front of my cabin door woke me up. I was lying on the floor of my bathroom with that door open so I could see across to my bed. There was just enough moonlight for me to see a hand reach around and lift the chair out of the way. The locks on this boat were ridiculous. A tall man came in silently and looked over at the bed where I had arranged pillows and blankets under the sheet to appear like I was asleep and facing the wall. Old hat, right? Whatever works, I say. The travel bag was hanging from a bedpost.

He stepped swiftly to the bed, raised his arm, and came down with something that went Thwack! on the pillow that was supposed to be my head. It made me flinch. He realized his mistake in half a second and spun around in time to get my foot in his mouth. He fell on the bed and I jumped on him, reaching around to get my arm across his throat. The s.o.b. flexed his overgrown shoulders, broke my grip, and whacked me backwards with an elbow to my chest. I stumbled over the chair, but recovered enough to pick it up and cream him with it. Good ol' chair didn't break because it was made of metal. I didn't have time to give a victory cry, though, 'cause his partner hit me on the back of the neck with something terribly hard and heavy. I went down paralyzed, but still conscious. Couldn't even raise my arms to avoid smashing my nose against a wastebasket, also metal. I saw them pick up the vinyl bag and beat it out of there and there wasn't anything I could do to stop them.

However, I did manage to crawl out on deck in time to see the two of them jump into the launch that had pulled alongside and sped away. No one else on the whole damn boat had stirred an inch. I only had enough strength left to smile before I went to sleep right there.

A deck hand found me in the morning and helped me to my cabin, and the captain came in to see how I was and get his binoculars back. He didn't seem overly concerned about the incident itself. "The River holds no more surprises for me," he said. One of the few really placid men I've met.

By noon the paralysis had worn off enough to leave me with no more than a stiff neck, and we docked in Bamako at three. I looked over the crowd of pushing, laughing, yelling colorful people and didn't see anyone I knew, or anyone I didn't want to know. I got off the boat carrying a suitcase and my precious brown vinyl bag and took a taxi to the Grand Hotel across from the railroad station. There I checked in, took a shower, and walked to the station to buy a ticket for Dakar. The next train was scheduled to leave at eight the following morning, which meant that it might get going by ten or eleven. I had time to make some more purchases for my business. There was no sense in hiding my presence in Bamako. The word would already be going out. So I strolled over to the central market where most of the artisans are to say hello to old trader friends and pick up some amber beads and assorted masks and statues. I did get one nice six-foot Mossi "guardian god" and a couple excellent *chiwara* antelopes. While hunched over in a bargaining session for some gold ear pendants I heard a familiar American voice.

"Well I'll be... Lee Loring! I didn't know you were in town."

"Hi, Bill. Nice to see you. I just got in." It was William Whitney, First Secretary of the U.S. Embassy. I had helped him negotiate a trade agreement a couple years back and we had been friends since. Usually I stayed at his place while I was in Bamako. "How's Carla and the kids?"

"Carla's fine, but lonely. We sent the kids off to Switzerland this year. The school situation here is getting pretty bad. How come you didn't let us know you were here?"

"It's just an overnight stop. Didn't want to trouble you."

"Hey, you're never any trouble." Shows you how much you can know about your friends. "Look, why don't you have dinner with us at least. We're entertaining some bigwig grain expert and his wife from the States tonight and you might as well get in on a free meal. 'Sides, you might be able to tell him some things about Africa that I don't dare. What say I pick you up at seven? You're staying at the hotel, right?"

I had been on the verge of refusing adamantly. Dining with Stateside wheels who think they can solve all of Africa's problems after a week's stay is way, way down on my preference list of things to do. However, his last sentence stopped me. I turned and gave him a big, slow grin. He was a good political man. Kept a straight face. "Sure, Bill, I'll be glad to come. But I'll get my own way over. See you at seven."

"Good. Carla will be happy to see you. Bye."

Will you really be happy to see me, Carla? I wondered. After that last nocturnal dip in the pool when I wouldn't help you off... But no, let's not be unkind to my friends. I had problems enough in the present. Now that everybody knew I was in town and staying at the Grand Hotel, I might as well go whole hog and try to get some advantage out of it. I called the Director of Tourism, Jean Babemba, and invited him for a drink at *Les Trois Caimans,* a riverside restaurant. Not surprisingly, he wasn't surprised to hear from me.

"Well, Jean," I said as we settled into a booth, "how's the tourist business?"

"Growing every day, Lee. How's the black market artifact business?"

I looked around in mock terror. "Watch it, Jean. You still want me to come around and buy up the cheap junk you can't palm off on visitors, don't you?"

He laughed, a hearty, rolling, bubbling laugh that came from somewhere out of his massive gut and sent ripples along his bald head. "Of course, of course. Our economy would break down without you. What have you gotten this time?"

"Oh, just bits and pieces. Nothing you wouldn't want to let out of the country. I may even come around and have one of your boys stamp them 'authentic' for me." He laughed again, so I dug a bit. "I'm getting more interested in Chinese art, though. Heard there was a Chinese cultural mission in the country. Will they be bringing in any good pieces?"

His brow clouded over and he didn't say anything more until after the waiter had served the drinks. Then he took a long sip of J.W. and said to the table, "They have people traveling all over the country to visit our best artisans and dancers for a possible show in Peking. I think they'll be taking more out than they bring in."

"All over the country, huh? Must be a pretty good-sized mission."

Jean fidgeted with his glass. "Twenty-three, all told. Eighteen of them are here in Bamako. They make the rounds of the artisan stalls every day."

"Then I must be lucky. I picked up some good items today."

"They seem to be very selective. Mostly interested in masks. But they haven't bought anything yet." For the first time since the drinks arrived, Jean looked me full in the face. "I'd suggest you don't deal in masks for awhile, Lee. Just friendly advice."

"That's my business, Jean. I think instead I simply won't deal with the Chinese."

"That's a good idea, too." Jean swirled his drink and took another sip. "As a friend, I'm asking you not to cause any trouble for Mali. We need the Chinese right now. They want something. We don't know what it is, but we won't stop them from getting it."

"Jean, I wouldn't dream of doing anything to hurt

Mali. I think of it as my second home."

"Perhaps, but I don't think you'd want to make it your permanent one."

It was my turn to laugh, but it came out weak and unconvincing. "Uh, Jean, do you intend to help them get what they want?"

He smiled broadly. "How can we, if we don't know what it is? And anyway, although we need the Chinese, we can't afford to play favorites. Except in your case. Remember that the cultural mission has diplomatic immunity... and you don't. I'm glad you're leaving tomorrow."

"Ouch! Your hints are like javelins. And my privacy here is nil." I checked my watch. It was ten to seven. I rose and left a bill on the counter. "Thanks, Jean, for whatever. I won't forget you at Christmas, if I live till then."

"Don't be too glum, Lee. I also hear you have more friends in Mali than you realize. *Au revoir.*"

Whitney's house was only a few blocks from the restaurant, so I walked. A low pall of smoke hung over the city, visible about eight or ten feet off the ground through the scattered street lights. It was Bamako's own form of smog that gathered every night about the same time, and it was caused by thousands of outdoor cooking fires. The fact that it was good smoke rather than hydrocarbons made the night seem cozy instead of oppressive. At Whitney's house a servant let me in and I walked up to where Bill and Carla and their guests were having drinks around the pool.

"Lee, come on in. Ibrahim, get Mr. Loring a Ricard."

"Lee, darling, I'm so glad you could come. We've missed you."

"Hi Bill, Carla. Nice to be here again."

Carla came up and kissed me on the cheek, then took me by the arm and led me to the others. I was turned on by the touch of her. And her smell. And her looks. She did a pretty good job on all my senses. I think her ancestors were Portugese. Carla had long, glossy black hair and very fair skin, much of which was showing around the corners of the sleeveless red sheath she was wearing. It was a fun-filled struggle to keep my eyes away from her oh-so-low neckline. What curious games we civilized mortals play, all centered around Let's Pretend. She was playing "Let's Pretend I Don't Really Notice That You Are Excited By The Fact That My Tits Are Hanging Halfway Out Of My Dress," and I had to play "Let's Pretend That Your Partially Bare Body And Musky Perfume Doesn't Bother Me." Bill was going along with it, too. He was playing, "Let's Pretend I'm So Secure That I Don't Care." Even the guests had joined in. They were playing, "See No Evil, Hear No Evil, Speak No Evil."

"...Jim and Margaret Thrasher," Carla was saying. "Jim is a grain expert from the Department of Agriculture. Mr. Loring deals in African *objets d'art*." We shook hands all around and I sat down where Ibrahim had put my drink.

"Oh say, let me take your travel bag," offered Bill. "I'll hang it in the closet."

I hugged the vinyl closer. "No thanks, I'd rather keep it with me. Bought some rare stuff today and I'll feel better if it's within reach."

"Can we see it?" asked Carla.

"Like to," I smiled, "but it's all wrapped." I turned to the guests. "Well, Mr. Thrasher, what kind of grain are you expert in?" Thrasher was a red-faced, sparse-haired, "beefy" man (if you don't mind my using that term for someone in the Agriculture Department) who looked like he had spent most of his life on a farm. Mrs. Thrasher looked like... well, like she ought to be the wife of Mr. Thrasher.

"Sorghums, son. Sorghums and millet. Been at it since I was knee-high to a grasshopper." Oh God, a hearty "down-home" type. Had he really said that? I reminded myself never to forgive Bill for inviting me.

Thrasher proceeded to tell me all about sorghum and the new varieties that he thought should be introduced to Mali which had lusher leaf growth and heavier heads and would make far better fodder than the local kinds. "We'll get those cattle so fat even the Maliens won't recognize them."

He was still going at it at the dinner table. Bill sent me a desperate look. Carla just nuzzled my foot with hers. "Mr. Thrasher," I interrupted, "how long have you been in Africa?"

"Five days, five whole days. Long enough to see that this place really needs some shaking up by American know-how."

"Has anyone bothered to tell you that the Africans don't feed sorghum and millet to their cattle?"

"What! Then what in hell do they do with it?"

"They eat it. And make beer with it. 'Bout the same way we use corn."

"Well I'll be bit by a bee!" I cringed, Bill

concentrated on his food, Carla coughed into her napkin, and Mrs. Thrasher smiled nervously.

That good lady broke the ensuing silence by saying, "Tell us about African art, Mr. Loring. It must be fascinating." And the rest of the evening was mine.

Toward eleven the Thrashers decided they'd better get to bed, even though they would have loved to hear more about the subtle differences in *ibeji* doll carving between the various Yoruba villages, and I reluctantly agreed that it was getting late. They were staying at the *Motel de Bamako* near the airport and Bill offered to drive me to the hotel after taking them home. "Stay and have another drink with Carla and I'll be right back." Carla, naturally, thought that was a good idea. Bill was still playing "I'm Secure" and Carla was onto "Let's Pretend We're Just Good Friends And Have No Intention Of Screwing Before Bill Gets Back," but I was through with games. It suddenly came to me that I was honestly too tired. Also, the vision of me leaping into my pants as Bill pulled into the driveway didn't appeal. Much to Carla's chagrin and Bill's relief I insisted on walking back to the hotel. It was only about twenty blocks and I enjoyed night walks. I figured there was less danger for me outside than inside. In a way I was right. In another way I was wrong.

It was nice walking along the semi-dark tree-lined avenues. Temperature was in the low seventies, no people were out, and there were very few sounds. I didn't even bother thinking. Just let my body enjoy the sensory experience of the surroundings.

It was in the area called *Bozola* that my sensory

experience began to change dramatically. Cars had been rare, but I still didn't pay any attention to the one that turned into the street I was on. Until it crossed over on the wrong side and headed straight for me. Sheee-it, I thought. I should have played games with Carla. I leaped behind a tree and the car skidded to a halt, trapping me in its lights. Two doors slammed and I rushed to the side to find myself facing five grim-faced Chinese. I turned around and five or six more were blocking my exit. Oh, how I would like to tell you that I attacked in both directions at once with iron nerves, slashing hands and flailing feet. But that isn't what happened. I stood where I was and shouted AU SECOURS! (which means HELP! in case you took Spanish instead of French in high school).

Then the miracle took place. Logical skeptic that I am, I shall always remember it as a miracle. From out of the darkness twenty-five or so blacks came running and attacked the Chinese. I recall thinking that New York was never like this. It was an amazing fight to watch. The Chinese were skilled in formal hand combat, but the blacks were tough and enthusiastic street-fighters. Also, they outnumbered the Chinese by more than two to one. One Chinese was super-good, though, and had fended off four attackers. But five more rushed him and bore him down, then picked him up and slammed his head against the tree. I won't describe what it sounded like in case you happen to be eating a sandwich while you are reading this. A few minutes more and all the Chinese were down and out. About half the blacks were still standing and helping their fellows up. One big fella came up to me and I wondered whether I would get the Foreign Legion next time I called out, but he only took my hand and gave me the sign of the Followers of the Mask. "In Bamako you are under the protection of the Arjunate," he said quietly, "but when you leave you are on your own again. May the Mask bring you luck, brother. We count on you." Then he and the others slipped away.

There were no incidents the rest of the way to the hotel and I was grateful for that. I was content not having any more occasions for the mask to prove its worth as a good luck charm. At the hotel I went straight to my room, flipped on the light, and flipped it off again. What had happened to my luck?

"Hello, Lee," came Rocky's smooth voice. "Did you think you'd get rid of us so easy?"

"Well, I sort of had hopes. What are you doing in my bed?"

"Waiting for you. Turn the light back on."

"Not on your life. Not until you put some clothes on."

She laughed like jungle drums. "Darla never told me you were a prude."

"Not a prude, just prudent. There's a difference. Okay, what happened? Where are Sami and Darla?"

The sheets rustled and I couldn't help thinking of the limbs that were doing the rustling. I felt like forming myself into a posse to catch the rustlers (oooh, that was bad. I apologize.) No kidding, though. Rocky dressed was fabulous. Undressed she was outtasight. And I wanted to keep her that way for the time being. "Dont' get out of bed," I said hurriedly. "Tell me right from there."

"All right. Darla was a little put out when the plane took off without you." Flame-throwing furious was probably more like it. "Sami was worried that you had been taken off and I was simply puzzled. Anyway, by the time we landed at Bamako it was decided that Darla and Sami would go on to Dakar with the mask and I would get off to search for you. You sure took your time in coming."

"Go on." I couldn't see her, but I knew she was out of bed because her voice sounded closer. In a moment I'd have to turn on the light to protect myself. I didn't find out about her knives till much later, you see.

"At the airport Darla and Sami had to go through customs before boarding the plane for Dakar. Usually there's no problem leaving the country, but this time there were some French officials with the customs officer and when Darla checked through they confiscated the bag with the mask. I was already out of the boarding area so I could see that she and Sami were putting up a great argument until the customs officer called two policemen over and they were herded onto the plane at gunpoint. Then the Frenchmen took the bag and left. I followed them in a cab to the French Embassy. Then I got to wondering what I would do if I were you, so I waited for you. Watched you check in the hotel this afternoon and got the clerk to let me in as your *companion du nuit*." Her voice was much closer now. "Aren't you glad I'm here?"

I switched on the light. Rocky was three feet in front of me, stark naked. Was she ever naked. I mean really naked. I mean, some women take their clothes off and they are just nude. But Rocky was naked. It sent a ripple through my loins. Her breasts were impossibly high and tipped with dark rose. Her waist was too slender to believe, and her hips... omigod her hips were... enough to make a strong man fall to his knees. I was just a tiny bit stronger than that, due, no doubt, to my many years of healthful exercise and clean living.

"Rocky," I gargled. I cleared my throat and tried again. "Rocky," I rasped, "please, uh, I mean, what about Demba? Don't tempt me too far, okay? I'm just a man."

"And I'm just a woman, Lee. With all the needs and desires of my sex. I like Demba, but we have no commitments to each other, and he's a thousand miles away. You're here. I'm here. And there's only a little bit of air between us. Let's do what we were made for."

I've failed to describe her body. How can I describe her voice? It was the purr of a lioness, the deep call of a female animal in a moonlit forest, the siren song of a Lorelei. Instead of sharpening my wits that idea only added to my entrancement. She was dangerous, deadly, I knew that. But I let myself go with that ancient cry of the human male singing in my head: What a way to die!

I died several little deaths that night. Now, I have been around the world and consider myself somewhat of a gourmet (some would say gourmand) in sexual matters, but Rocky opened up a whole new world for me. For instance, the Ghanian Grip was totally new to me, and I had only heard dim rumors of the Ivory Coast Hipswing. And the Dahomeen

Double. Wow! I hadn't even known that existed. She showed me all those and more. We ended shortly before dawn in a Zulu Twist and I fell into an exhausted sleep.

On opening my eyes I was mildly surprised that I was still alive, more surprised to find my vinyl bag and its contents intact, and shocked to see Rocky walk in with coffee and croissants. "You're still here," I said stupidly.

She looked down at herself. "Most of me," she answered happily. "I think I lost a few pounds."

"That's not what I mean. I thought you'd be gone with the goods."

"Lee, I'm disappointed in you. What a suspicious nature. You hired me to help you, remember?"

"Mmmm," I mumbled around a croissant. "Could it also be that you wanted to make sure of getting the real mask?"

"Well, there's no sense in having me guard a fake one."

I gestured to the bag on the floor. "There it is. You could have taken it."

Cat-like chuckle. "Yes, I could have. But you are so tricky sometimes. I thought it would be best to stay with you until you deliver. I only want to help, you know." She sat on the bed, put an arm around me and kissed me.

Finally, I broke away. "No more this morning. I have a train to catch."

"*We* have a train to catch. I'm booked, too. Same compartment, as a matter of fact."

"Wonderful," I said unenthusiastically. "Okay, at least let me get dressed in private. I'll meet you downstairs. How much time do we have?"

"An hour before departure time."

"I'll be down in thirty minutes."

Rocky looked slowly around the room. I knew she had checked the place out and was wondering if I could have hidden the real mask in a place she had overlooked.

"It's in the bag, sweetheart. Right under your nose."

She gave me a look that said she didn't know whether to believe me or not. "All right. Thirty minutes." She left.

Most of the items I had bought in Timbuctu had been sent off on the plane, but I had handcarried a few from Ousmane in the suitcase. I looked and they were all there. Three ostrich eggs decorated with leather trim, two figurines of pregnant women, some gold earrings and silver ankle bracelets, and a largish, rather nondescript mask in the Senufo style. I checked the vinyl bag and the glitter of metal told me that mask hadn't been removed. So I showered, shaved, dressed and went down to meet Rocky.

If you have never waited in the train station at Bamako, I don't recommend it. The crowd is enormous, noisy, smelly and panicky at the thought that the train might leave without them. Rocky and I were standing behind a large woman with two trunks balanced precariously on her head. Every few moments she would turn her head to one side and spit, then do the same on the other side. In this way she assured herself of elbow room. Her neck was so agile that the protected cone of space behind her was very narrow. We couldn't move anywhere else because of the crowd and each time the woman spat the trunks would tilt backwards enough to make me fear for my skull. At long last the train pulled in and the crowd surged forward. The only trouble was that the big iron gates to the platform were hinged to swing inward. The train officials tried to push the gates in while the crowd tried to push them out and we might have still been there except for an experienced old codger who opened a smaller exit further down. The crowd had pushed us to its outer edge, so we dashed for the small exit while the crowd was still trying to crush itself. We got to our first class compartment, a six by six stall with two bunks and a sink, and an hour and a half later the train was on its way.

At twelve-thirty I went to the dining car ahead of Rocky, who was adjusting her turban, and what should I find but...

"Mr. Loring! Why what a fine surprise to see a fellow American aboard this godforsaken excuse for a train. Thought I'd take a look at the countryside to see how we can improve it. Even if they're going to eat the sorghum themselves they've got a right to quality, right?"

"Hello, Mr. Thrasher, Mrs. Thrasher. Going all the way to Dakar?" I crossed my fingers.

"No, no, just to Kayes, before the border. Got a car waiting for us there." Thank God for little favors. "I see you're still carrying your valuable cargo. I'd give a pretty penny to see what's in there."

Was that an offer? Maybe Thrasher wasn't what he said he was. "How much do you have in mind?" I asked.

"What? Oh, I was just joshing, son, just joshing. Figure of speech. C'mon and join us for lunch. I'd like to get your opinion on my plan for increasing productivity. These lazy nig-..." Mrs. Thrasher discreetly kicked him. "Uh, I mean these poor people don't know the first thing about good farming."

I was in no mood to be entertained by Thrasher's farm policies. "Thanks, really, but I'm waiting for my wife."

"Good, good, she can join us. Sit right down here and we can solve the world's problems while the ladies chit-chat."

You asked for it, fella. I sat down and the waiter brought us the fixed menu—lentils and beef chunks. We had just started to dig in when Rocky entered the car. I waited till she was alongside and then I stood up.

"Mr. and Mrs. Thrasher, I'd like you to meet my wife, Abigail." Curious phenomenon. I have said that Thrasher was red-faced. He surprised me by increasing that color several shades as he choked on his beans.

He kept on choking even though Mrs. Thrasher and I whacked him on the back. He finally waved us away feebly and staggered out of the dining car still hacking and gasping with his wife right behind. For the next three meals they avoided us like we had contagious malaria.

Rocky and I sat down and laughed our heads off. "Abigail," she said, wiping her eyes, "why Abigail?"

"Why not?"

The trip continued smoothly after that, till just before we reached Kayes. No spies seemed to be lurking about, and as far as I could see the train was free of Chinese, Russians and Frenchmen. I was standing at the bar finishing off a late afternoon tonic and worrying about the next stage of the game when Mrs. Thrasher joined me.

"Mr. Loring, I'd like to apologize for the way my husband has been acting."

"That's okay. Didn't mean to shock him."

Her eyes twinkled. "Well, I think you did, but it doesn't matter. Where is your companion?" She didn't say wife.

"Taking a nap." My inner alarm went off.

"Harold, my husband, is in the john. The food doesn't seem to agree with him. Could I talk to you alone in my compartment for a few minutes?"

"That sounds compromising."

"Don't worry. This old lady won't try to seduce you. I'm interested in the contents of your travel bag. The real contents. It will be worth your while."

"All right, let's hear what you have to say."

He went to her compartment and she locked the door. Then she reached into her bra and pulled out a card that said she worked for the CIA. My eyebrows tried to climb past my ears. "Harold really is my husband and he is a grain expert, but he doesn't know I've been with the Agency for years. What you are carrying is very important to the foreign policy of your country. Actually, it would be your patriotic duty to turn it over to us, but I've read your profile and your sense of duty appears to need material stimulation."

"Nicely put, little ol' lady."

"I'm prepared to pay you ten thousand dollars in

U.S. currency right now for what's in the bag."

I reached for the door lock. "Sorry, ma'm, I'm delivering it to a party in Dakar who is offering fifty thousand."

And so began the go round. She argued that cash in hand was worth more than a promise. I argued that gambling on high stakes was my way of life. She argued that the American Government was the only one that could be trusted not to misuse what I had. I argued that Watergate led me to think otherwise. She argued that incriminating documents could be planted which would get me kicked out of Senegal permanently and land me a ten-year prison term in the States. I settled at last for twenty thousand Federal Reserve notes of legal tender.

"Do you mind if I look at what I'm buying?"

"Of course not. I can't afford to have an unsatisfied customer." I handed her the bag.

She opened it up and looked inside. "It fits the description. I hope they know what they're doing." She faced away from me and lifted her skirt. When she turned back she held a stack of bills.

I took them. "Do you mind if I check them?" She grimaced, but nodded consent. I held them up to the overhead light. They were good enough to pass in the black market and that was all I cared about. I pocketed them and unlocked the door. "Nice doing business with you, Mrs. Thrasher. Have a pleasant stay in Africa. Oh, and you can keep the bag."

That evening I watched the Thrashers get off at Kayes and head for a waiting Jeepster. Bless you, Ousmane, I said silently.

On we rolled into the night. Somewhere in the

middle of it we were awakened for passport and luggage checks at the Senegal border. I had to go to the baggage car to open the packages of stuff I had bought in Bamako, but everything passed okay. We had to wait outside our compartment while a border official sprayed everything with kerosene to kill off all the Malien germs and then we were permitted to go back inside and slosh through the oily liquid that flooded the floor. The stink made sleep a bit difficult, but we eventually drifted into it.

Around seven the next morning we pulled into Tambacounda, a sleepy town in eastern Senegal that had once been the big halfway stop for French travelers in the days before commercial airplanes. Rocky was already up and dressed. Even though I had promised her a share of the sale she was barely speaking to me. She had thrown a fit when I told her about it after leaving Kayes. "I'm going to the dining car for coffee," she said curtly.

"Be with you in a minute." I counted to fifty before opening my suitcase and taking out the Senufo-style mask. It tingled when I tucked it under my jacket. I got off the train and walked casually toward the station hotel. I was halfway there when Rocky spotted me from the dining car.

She lowered a window and shouted, "Where are you going?"

"Just stretching my legs," I shouted back. I carefully maintained my pace until I entered the door to the restaurant. Then I looked around frantically. Where was he?

"Here I am, *patron*." He'd been sitting by the door and I'd missed him.

I realized I'd been holding my breath and I let it blow out. Sarr was another driver of mine. As soon as I had checked into the hotel in Bamako I had called Aletha and told her to send Sarr out to meet me at Tambacounda with my Land Rover. "Where are the keys?"

"Right here, *patron*." He held them out and I grabbed them.

"Got your ticket?"

"Yes, *patron*."

"Get on the train!" And I ran out the front of the hotel. What made me run was the fact that I had looked out the window and seen Rocky running toward the restaurant. It hurt that she didn't trust me. I jumped into my Rover and started it up. The safari job had been destroyed at Aoudaghost, but this short baby was every bit as tough. I gunned out of the parking lot and saw a chilling sight in the rearview mirror. Another Rover had pulled out after me, but had stopped short when Rocky came tearing out of the hotel. Rocky climbed aboard and now they were following me. A red flame in the driver's seat told me it was Darla. The Amazons were on my tail.

I headed south on the road to Kedougou, a winding, twisting, bumpy mound of dirt. The needle on the speedometer rose to fifty miles an hour, a highly dangerous speed for this kind of road. The roadbed was corrugated and above thirty you kind of float over the humps. At my speed it was very much like driving on ice. It took all my skill to keep from drifting into a ditch or taking a spin. I hoped the dust would force Darla to drop behind, but every so often I caught a glimpse of her moving up on me. Rovers aren't easy beasts. She was a damn good driver. I gained on the curves and lost on the straightaways.

Where was I going? To a spot that appeared in my dream. Foolish? You said it! But that's where I was going. It was a circle of columns carved out of lava rock and so ancient that there weren't even any local traditions about who had made them. It was said only that they were inhabited by ghosts. There were a fair number of them in Senegal, mostly way off the beaten path. The one I was heading for was even more out of the way than the others, and unlike the majority it had a slingshot-shaped column in the center. My objective.

I geared down for the turn-off and whipped my mechanical animal into it. The going was slower now out of necessity, but not by much. Roads had never sullied this stretch. Across streambeds, up steep hills, over rock outcroppings and through woods the two Rovers raced like turtles. It got rougher and rougher. I had it on four-wheel drive all the time now and occasionally had to slip down into low range. I don't think another kind of vehicle could have made it. Darla was further behind, but my tracks were easy to follow. There weren't any others.

I babied the Rover over a last hillock and there it was. A circle of stones in the middle of nowhere. Weeds had grown up all around it, but not in the center. There it was like someone had swept it clean. I stopped and got out some thirty or forty yards from it. I took my pocket knife and ran it along the edge of the Senufo-style mask where I had sealed it with some of Ousmane's black wax. Two halves of thin light wood popped apart and there lay the Mask of God, its gold and silver gleaming in the sunlight.

It would have been normal to be afraid of what I had to do, but I was beyond normalcy at that point. I had no thoughts, no feelings. Only an urgent need to move forward. I had the Mask of God. And now I had to eat its heart.

The sound of the other Rover barely reached me, and I was only dimly aware of what happened next. Darla jumped down and pointed something at me with both hands.

"Stop right there, Lee. This is a gun and I'll kill you if I have to." It was noise from another world. I kept moving. There was a metallic sound like a hammer being cocked.

Rocky had jumped down, too, and was facing Darla with her hand raised. "Drop it, Darla. You're dead if you don't. He has to finish this."

Darla's voice was strained, but she kept the gun on me. "Rocky! What is this? We're sisters! The Lorelei wants that mask!"

Though I was fast losing touch with my surroundings, I remember faint surprise at the sobs when Rocky spoke. "We're sisters, and I love you. And the Lorelei. But Lee has to destroy that mask. Before Sami and I left for Timbuctu Demba asked me to visit some relatives who were supposed to know something about the secret society that has been ruled by the mask. When I got there they took me to that Lebou sorcerer we were trying to find. Only he isn't a sorcerer. He's... something else. Anyway, the mask is—how did he put it—out of control. He showed me what will happen if it's misused for any length of time. I can't explain it, but I've *seen* it. I don't want that to happen to the Lorelei. Or to you. And if I must I'll kill you to save you from becoming..." The rest was incoherent.

With my last shreds of awareness I saw Darla drop the gun and the two women run to embrace each other. After that I was gone. From what I heard later I climbed the slingshot and stood with one foot on each prong. Then I raised my face to the sun and covered it with the mask. From that moment the accounts differ. Darla says I glowed like a neon bulb and that the ground seemed to tremble like an earthquake. Rocky says that blue flames shot out from every part of my body and that the ground in the center of the circle turned to a bubbling liquid. My only memory is of... But that's too far out. You wouldn't believe me anyway. The women did agree on one thing. During the spectacle the mask crumbled in my hands, metal and all, and the particles were apparently blown away by the wind before they touched the ground. So be skeptical. I don't blame you.

I came to with Darla and Rocky hovering over me outside the circle. They claim I climbed down and walked out under my own power, then fainted dead away. Darla had my head in her lap and Rocky was patting my cheeks. I was just beginning to enjoy myself when I heard:

"Well done." It was Baba N'Dow. Don't ask me how he got there. For my part I'd rather not know. "The mask is destroyed, but the society lives. The world has been saved from this danger, even though it will face others. The lion's lair has been avoided, but what of the cobra's bite? We move on from crisis to crisis, for that is the way of learning, and without learning, what is there to life? No crisis, no learning; no learning, no life; no life, no death; no death, no life. Have patience with an old man's babble. Your training is not over, Lee Loring, but you may not be called on again for some time. Until then, enjoy life, for the only alternative is not to enjoy it and no sensible man would make that choice. Nor would any woman." With that he turned and walked off into the brush. The day was hot and heat waves were flickering up from the ground. That's what must have made it seem like he faded away. Or so I hope.

Postscript

Salif found his way back. The two Touaregs who bore him off fell into an argument over profits in the hills by Ras el Ma and while they were stabbing each other he managed to slip away. A Bambara family found him, gave him food and shelter in return for help on their farm, and gradually he worked his way to Dakar. I got word to El Kerim about his nephew Daoud and, though greatly saddened, he was grateful enough to send me a magnificent chest inlaid with copper and silver. Demba finally got his private parts back in working order and flew to Paris for a special conference on investigative techniques. Sami changed his office decor to an Alpine meadow and turned his air conditioner down to 65 degrees so that you had to wear winter clothes when you paid a visit. And I wasn't bothered by anyone asking for their money back for unusable merchandise. All my museum orders were filled and the only obligation outstanding was a visit to Togo the following week for a friend in some kind of trouble. Life was looking easy when Aletha sinuously slinked into my office.

"Monsieur Loring, it is time for a vacation."

"All right, Aletha, there's not much happening. How long will you be gone?"

"*Non, non, Monsieur*, we must go together. You told me the old man said that life is learning, so we are going to learn something new."

Kiddingly, I said, "Aletha, there's nothing new under the sun."

"Then we will do it in the dark. It is called . . ." She shouted to the outer office. "What do you call that again?"

Rocky and Darla slithered through the door and said in unison, "Quadrangular Fling."

Zing!

AMY JEAN

Lorinda Hagen

a chilling tale of reincarnation...

Christopher Lewis was crushed by the death of his beautiful wife, Amy Jean. But a spark of hope began to burn within him when she called to him from beyond the grave. She promised she would return, and she and Christopher would be together—*forever!*

From that moment on, Christopher searched for Amy Jean. His thirteen-year search led him to some of the most controversial psychics in the country—and to one girl who became so entangled in his web of obsession that her life would never be the same.

...in the haunting tradition of AUDREY ROSE

HOUSES OF HORROR

TERRIFYING TALES OF HAUNTED HOUSES

Hans Holzer

noted parapsychologist and psychic researcher

Have you ever come home and wondered what might be lurking up the stairs, in the dark of the corridor where the lights don't reach?

Thousands of people who live in old houses—and some who live in modern homes—have come face to face with *something* that wasn't in their purchase contract.

Neither victim nor ghost escapes the consequences of their being put in each other's way. The victims may move on to new surroundings—but they will never forget the horror they have experienced. And the ghost will go on re-enacting its final compulsion until the house is pulled down around it—or even *beyond*.

"These case histories of haunted houses are all true stories . . . believers should love this collection."
—*Publishers Weekly*

LEISURE BOOKS　　　　　　　　　　　　1143-3/$2.25

LILY DALE

Paul Tabori

A SPELL-BINDING CHILLER

Who was Lily Dale? A mystic? A prophet? A fraud? She seduced the entire world into believing that her psychic powers were real. Yet when she accidentally summoned up the very spirits she had scorned for so long, Lily found herself facing the terrifying wrath of supernatural forces which she was utterly unable to control.

Price: $2.75
0-8439-2007-6
pp. 256

Category: Occult

**In the far future,
an interstellar pleasure ship
is launched on a voyage of death!**

STARBRIGHT
DAMON CASTLE

There are fun and games on board for mid-flight entertainment. And suddenly, there is a horrible accident. And blood. And death. And then the alien armies strike.

SCIENCE FICTION

0-8439-2058-0

$2.50